A Pigeon Lake Novel

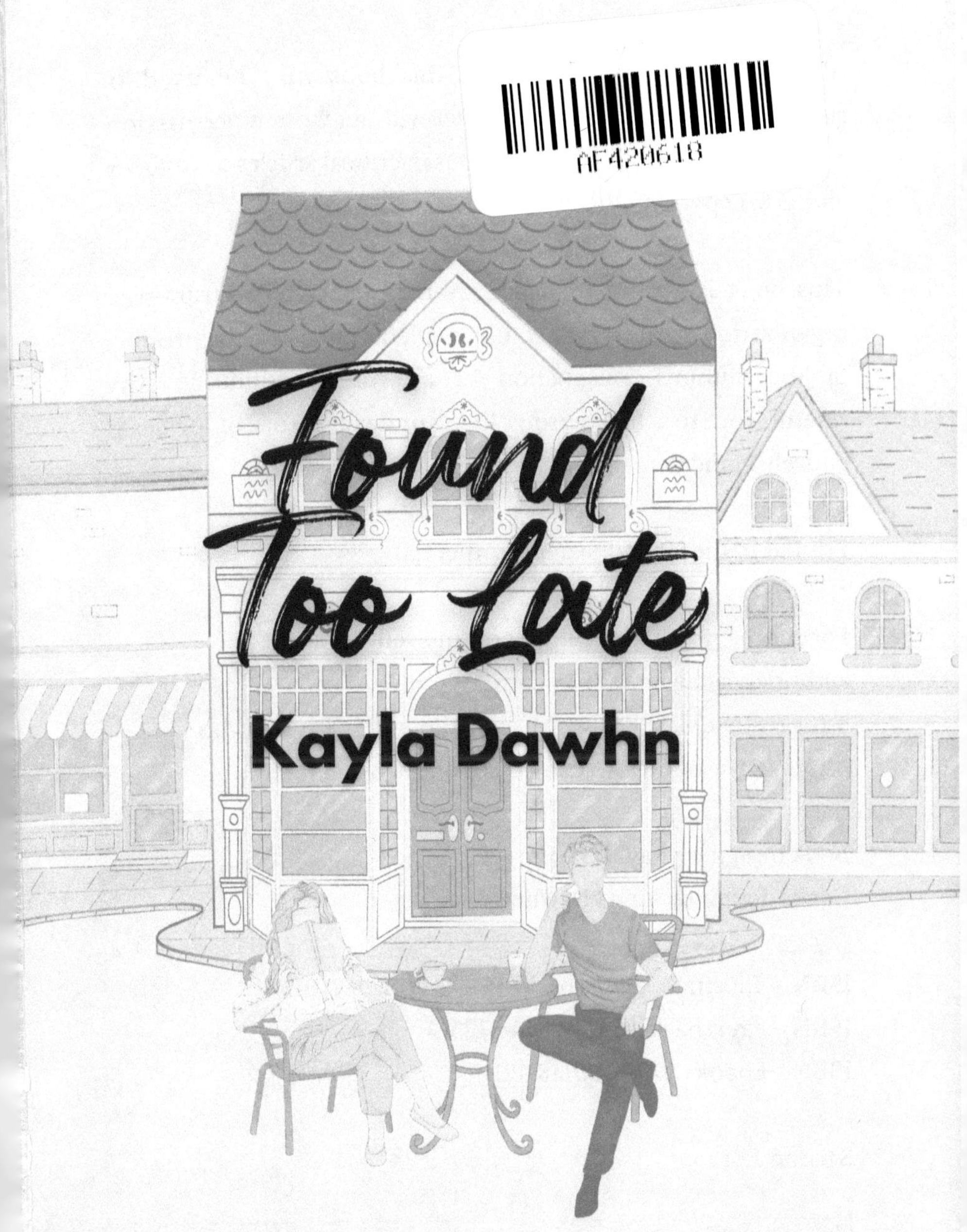

Contents

PLAYLIST
Found Too Late

▶	**WILD ONES** Jessie Murph, Jelly Roll	2:21
▶	**BUY MYSELF A CHANCE** Randy Rogers Band	3:40
▶	**CARRY ON** Pat Green	4:56
⏸	**PICK ME UP** Gabby Barrett	2:48
▶	**BIG ENERGY** Latto	2:52
▶	**RIDIN' ROADS** Dustin Lynch	3:24
▶	**WORST WAY** Riley Green	3:40
▶	**HOW DOES IT SOUND** Dylan Schneider	2:41
▶	**BETTER FOR ME** Max McNown	3:13
▶	**NEXT THING YOU KNOW** Jordan Davis	2:54
▶	**STRAWBERRY WINE** Deanna Carter	4:51
▶	**YOU ARE IN LOVE** Taylor Swift	4:26
▶	**COUNTRY BOY'S DREAM GIRL** Ella Langley	3:04
▶	**BUY DIRT** Jordan Davis, Luke Bryan	2:47

Content Warnings

This book contains mature themes and language that may not be suitable for all readers. It includes explicit language and sexual content. Reader discretion is advised.

All pages that include explicit sexual content will include the 🌶 **symbol in the bottom right corner**, giving all readers the ability to read this book without the mature content if they choose.

Dedication

This is for the ones who *want* to fall for the good guy but always find themselves wanting that tattooed bad boy with a dirty mouth.

I give you Chase.

Chapter One

PROLOGUE
ABIGAIL, ONE YEAR AGO

tried to stop her. I really did, but I don't think there was anything I could have said to stop this trainwreck. My lifelong friend has finally stepped back into our small town after a self-imposed exile spanning seven long years, and we had no choice but to celebrate her arrival with a night out at Meryl's Bar.

Honestly, I missed her laugh more than I care to admit, and I longed to hear her weave those outrageous, impossible-to-believe stories that only she could tell. She had her own reasons to vanish – reasons that would've driven most people far away – but Macy was different: stubborn, fierce loyalty, my ride-or-die, the one person I could never allow to slip away.

We are crammed into a battered corner of the bar, all sticky tabletops, sputtering neon beer signs clinging to the wood-paneled walls like flickering specters, and an ever-present haze of stale smoke, split whisky, and worn-leather boots that lingered in the air. We clutch frosty beer bottles, fingertips slick with condensation, as a humid Texas breeze sweeps through the open doorway, carrying hints of scorching asphalt, mesquite smoke, and diesel exhaust. With our second round settling in our hands, we drove into the saga of her dramatic escape from New York City.

Then, out of the corner of my eye, a pack of local men swagger through the door: dusty Wranglers riding low, scuffed work boots, flannel sleeves rolled up above big, calloused forearms. They make a beeline for the bar rail, their heavy boots echoing in the cramped space like distant thunder. My stomach clenches as Macy and I both turn to face the brewing trouble. In that exact second, I knew it was coming – a trainwreck that no single word could derail.

None of these men are strangers – they have haunted Meryl's just like I have – and I've seen those rough features and rougher hands hovering around this bar more times than I can count. The moment Macy spots the seemingly impromptu oil-field convention, her eyes light up. She springs up immediately, making her silver bracelets clink in rhythm with her hand movements. She grabs both of my hands and drags me to my feet in one fluid motion. Her perfect, glossy lips curve into an invitation, when I cut her off mid-sentence.

"No, Mace," I say, my voice surprisingly firm. "I really don't think that's smart. Remember Jason? The disastrous date from a couple of weeks ago? I'd rather not see his cocky grin and wandering eyes again."

But best laid plans don't survive contact with Macy. What she didn't realize was that Jason wasn't whom I was honestly avoiding. No, I was sidestepping someone far more catastrophic to my calm: a tall, broad-shouldered man propped against the bar, half-shadowed by neon light. Chase Travers. The sight of him—amber beer bottle raised to full, pouty lips—sent a flip-flop through my insides. I couldn't look away as his strong throat bobbed with each swallow. The scruff along his jaw caught the neon glow, and those ice-blue eyes, piercing beyond the crowds, making my skin tingle.

Yet Macy's black boots click forward, and she bulldozes into the worst of all outcomes: Lucas, her ex, wandering in with the rogue crew. Precisely on cue, Macy barrels over, and I trail her like a reluctant shadow, my pulse hammering in my ears. Luke's smile as he crosses the threshold crackles through the air, charging the room. Some of the guys wave or slap him on the back, but Chase barely nods—an almost dismissive tilt of the head before his gaze drifts away.

Suddenly, we are surrounded by burly bodies, the heat from their work-roughened shoulders rolling over us like waves. Luke's sharp voice cut through the low thump of the jukebox, and Macy answers with slick venom. In an instant, every eye in the bar swivels toward us. I shrug, resigned to the volley of barbs and backhanded greetings, all while doing my best not to keep peeking at the man who'd stolen my attention. Chase stands apart from the chaos, and I feel the tug of his stormy gaze even before I dare to meet it.

Earlier, I'd been trying to talk up Jason - safe, predictable Jason - but Chase is a pure electromagnetism, a lightning bolt that leaves me raw with need. We have only shared a couple of spins on some dusty dance floor, but those stolen moments had cracked my composure. Now here he is again, jaw stubbled and stern, arms crossing over his sculpted chest that haunts my dreams. I'd always chalked his cold reserve up to single fatherhood - if anyone had a reason to keep emotions on a short leash, it was him. But I wonder: was that truly what made him so impenetrable?

Macy and Luke's voices rise until it sounds like a personal storm, and before I can catch my breath, they storm out the door, their bickering trailing off into the night like distant thunder. The door slams behind them with a definitive clap - the jukebox even stutters mid-beat. Everything goes still. Only then does Chase's stare drop down to me, deliberate and unflinching, making warmth bloom under my skin.

He leans in, voice low and gravelly. "Do you need a ride home tonight?"

His tone is clipped - impatient, almost - but I knew he meant it. I lift my bottle in a shaky shrug, nodding at the empty doorway. "Looks that way," I admit, voice a whisper. "I tried to stop her, but...you can see how that worked out." I gestured helplessly toward the exit, the last vestige of my bravado draining away.

Chase takes a slow sip, condensation trickling down the amber glass. I hold my breath until he sets it back on the bar. "I'm assuming that was his ex?" he asks, curiosity softening the edge of his tone. His offer takes me off guard. This isn't something he would typically offer without making me beg and plead that he doesn't leave me stranded somewhere.

"Yep," I say, forcing a wry smile. "Macy and Lucas. The one and only." My fingers find the beer label and begin spinning it in nervous circles, a subconscious attempt to steady my racing heart.

He leans forward, offering a smirk so rare it felt like sunshine breaking through clouds. "So, Jason - I heard you went out with him a couple of weeks ago?"

Heat flames my cheeks as I hold his gaze. His question is a tease, a test, and I file away the curve of his lips for future consideration. "I don't know, Chase," I shoot back with a giggle, trying to sound breezy. "How do you think it went? Guys, these days - am I right?"

Outside, a honk blares - a jarring punctuation to our semi-heated banter. We both jump, eyes flicking to the door, then back to each other. A silent joke passes between us.

"Well, cheers to that," I said, lifting my bottle in a mock toast.

Chase's demeanor shifts as if remembering he has to be broody instead of flirty. "One more, and I'll take you home." This is why I find him so confusing. We were just joking and borderline-joking, but in an instant, that man disappears and the grumpy one returns. Did I do or say something that brought back the version of him that I despise? The version of him that reminds me that he really can't stand me and makes me question if he forgot who he was talking to earlier in the conversation.

I nudged him playfully, leaning close enough to catch the faint scent of pine and sandalwood. "One more, then you take me home," I whisper, soft hope threading through my words. And so, we wait, two unspoken promises suspended in the hum of that sticky-floored bar, dreaming of the day when maybe he won't hate me.

Chapter Two

CHASE

The night air is cool and still as I pull out onto the deserted street, the truck's headlights cut through the darkness like twin searchlights. Inside the cab, the only sound is the steady hum of the engine and the soft rustle of my boots against the floor mat. Abigail sits beside me, her shoulder brushing mine, but between us lies an expansive silence that presses against my eardrums. I've driven her home after evenings out more times than I care to admit, yet each trip feels like a new apology for intruding on my own plans.

I hate that I volunteered before she even had a chance to blink at someone else - maybe that Jason guy she just went out with could have given her a ride home. He seems decent enough; it would've saved me this way-too-obliging drive if she'd just waved him over. Instead, I offered my help without a second thought. Now I stew over every foot-in-mouth comment I've made tonight, every awkward pause that stretched between us.

Abigail Kline is stunning in a way that seems unfair to the rest of the world. Under the dashboard light, her blonde curls bounce like sunbeams trapped in glass, and her green eyes - deep and luminous - catch stray shafts of light, glimmering with irritation. When she laughs, whatever room she is in fills with the bright, musical trill of her joy, and I'm reminded that she effortlessly steals every room's attention. Even now, parked beside a silent streetlamp, she commands attention like a spotlight commands the eye.

What drives me crazy is her relentless cheerfulness - everywhere except with me. She flings barbs and chirps a sarcastic retort at the drop of a hat, and I've gotten so used to sparring with her that it's almost comforting. Lucas even jokes that I've discovered her kryptonite: me. I wonder if she bottles up all her real frustrations just to unload them on me, like some twisted prizefight only we know we're in.

Meanwhile, my daughter, Charlotte - Charlie - floats through my mind like a distant star. Since her mother and I split up, I've had zero desire to date again. Every time I imagine bringing someone home, I taste that old knot of heartbreak. Over the years, she has noticed those perfect families at school, and I could feel her small, puzzled eyes on me. I've been her guardian, her protector, from the moment she was born. My life revolves around keeping her safe, and so I've convinced myself that introducing someone new would be too reckless. Reckless for her and me. Dating isn't something I want to try again; the pain when it doesn't work out is too much.

Charlie doesn't know exactly what kind of woman I'd be interested in, but that hasn't stopped her from pointing out every "cute girl" she sees, pressing me to ask them on dates. There's nothing more mortifying than a nine-year-old setting you up like you're a bewildered contestant on a reality show. At least my sister Bell fills in the motherly gaps: she's at every school play and parent-teacher night, braids Charlie's hair a hundred different ways, and promised to have the "girl talk" on the biology front. Some things a dad just can't handle.

My reverie shatters when I hear Abigail's voice, sharp and sudden. "Why are you mad now?" Her tone has shifted - no longer the peppy bar companion but an irritated stranger. We're stopped at a weathered stop sign, the truck idling as she fixes me with narrow-eyed disapproval.

I shift, surprised. "I was wondering how I'll feel when Charlie starts dating."

She laughs - a rich sound that echoes off the metal dashboard - and suddenly the truck feels too small. The stereo's glow picks out every angle of her face, illuminating her cheekbones and the fine lines of her smile. Then her slender fingers flick up to turn the volume higher, a silent veto of my declaration.

On reflex, I reach down and click the dial back. The low hum returns, and Abigail rolls her head back against the seat, exhaling a guttural sound of frustration. Her eyes are squeezed shut; her lips whisper something I can't catch. After a moment, she pulls her curls into a loose, high bun - stray wisps escaping like small rebellions - but doesn't bother tucking them in. Her gaze shifts to me, challenge burning in her green eyes. "Chase, what in the hell is your problem with me?"

"I don't have a problem - apart from having to drive you home." The words taste bitter, but I push them out anyway. I'd rather endure her glare than leave her stumbling down those few blocks alone.

When we pull into her driveway, she unbuckles so fast I hear the click before she shifts. She flings open the door, stomps down, and slams it behind her in one slick move. Then I hear it - a strangled, high-pitched scream that ricochets off the house. Confusion freezes me in place.

Her door swings open again, and I glimpse tears streaking her cheeks as she stalks toward the front entrance. I should let her run away, let her go sulk in her house, but I also remind myself that Macy may kill me if something happens to her best friend. "Abigail!" I yell after her.

She fumbles with her keys at the door, shoulders trembling. I cross the yard, heart pounding, and slip the key from her quivering fingers. The lock clicks under my practiced hand, and she bolts inside before I can say more.

But I can't leave it there. She's always ignoring me, but tonight her tears leave me unsettled. I follow her down the dim hallway into the kitchen, where she paces, still sniffling, still wincing. She wrestles with a tiny box of Band-Aids; they tumble onto the wooden floor, the pieces fluttering like wounded birds. She bends to pick them up, tears undercutting her frustration until she's practically gasping.

I stand there, watching her shiver from the pain, and then I scoop her up in my arms and set her down on that hard, chilly surface. She gasps from the bite of stone against her skin, and her sobs falter.

"Abigail, what happened?" My voice is harder and more apathetic than I intended - framed by annoyance instead of concern.

She blinks, startled by my tone. "Nothing, Chase. Really. I'm fine." She tries to stand, but I press her firmly back.

"Show me." I grab her hand toward me. She hesitates, then reveals a red, swollen fingertip. I blink at the rawness of it.

Without another word, I cross to her medicine cabinet, rifling out ointment, cotton swabs, and a bottle of Tylenol. I return and press her hand into my palm, squeezing a bead of salve onto her cut. The smell of antiseptic warms the space. "Keep this clean," I instruct quietly. "Don't let it get infected."

She nods, staring up at me, silent. I discard the empty wrappers in the trash and then, almost reluctantly, head back towards the door. From behind me, I hear her voice - soft, carrying across the kitchen. "Thanks, Chase."

I pause with my hand on the doorknob but say nothing. I simply close the door and step out into the night, the house lighting fading behind me.

Inside that quiet driveway, I linger for a moment, breathing in the cool air. Nice or irritated, it always ends the same: us locked in a stalemate of exasperation and unlikely concern. And somehow, I know - I'll do it again. In the same vein of thought, I remind myself that I'm doing it to save her from me rather than doing it to be mean.

Chapter Three

ABIGAIL
NOW

"**You do know** they are already married, right?" Chase's drawling voice drifts lazily behind me, his words a mix of exasperation and amusement. Even after years of being forced into the same group of friends through Luke and Macy, he still manages to find new ways to irritate me. The sound carries through the thick summer air as we make our way across Macy's parents' backyard, where magnolia trees weave slanted shadows across the emerald grass. In one hand, he dangles a half-used roll of clear tape; in the other, he grips a motley collection of craft supplies – bundles of pastel ribbon and a handful of silver safety pins. His arsenal of anxious helpfulness would almost be endearing if he weren't so insistent on reminding me, at every possible opportunity, of how ridiculous this situation is.

I am fully aware that having a second wedding may be too over the top, but I am so thankful that Macy came home and gave Lucas another chance that I don't care. If this is what they want to do to resolidify their marriage, then I will show up for them and do as they ask.

Late afternoon sunlight pours like honey over the well-manicured lawn and pristine rows of white folding chairs we arranged for the ceremony. A soft breeze carries the sweet scent of honeysuckle from the flower beds, and the air thrums with cicadas, their steady drone of the Texas summer's soundtrack. Despite the idyllic scene, I can't fully appreciate it with Chase standing mere feet away, muttering under his breath in a gravelly undertone like a reluctant wedding goblin.

Earlier, I became so frustrated with him that I asked him to go to the house and find me the pink screwdriver, insisting that all the other screwdrivers are broken and wouldn't be helpful. Of course, there is no pink screwdriver. I just needed him to shut up for five seconds and stop reminding me that we are decorating a wedding for a couple who are already married and now expecting their first child.

I pivot sharply, planting one hand on my hip while the other is in a half-exasperated, half-pleading arc. "Yes, Chase," I say, my voice as crisp as starched linen. I'm filled with forced patience while I try not to notice how the sun catches the stubble on his jawline and how much I want to feel it against my skin. "I do," I vocalize slowly as if I am explaining something complex to a child. "But sometimes when you have friends - not like this is an active concept for you - you still have to show up and help them out when needed." My tone is sharp as I attempt to give him a warning look, communicating that his grumbly antics are not helping me right now. "Even if what they need seems... unnecessary."

His eyes roll back at me so dramatically, I swear the earth's tectonic plates shift. "Abigail," he exaggerates, savoring the full form of my name like a secret weapon. He knows how much I hate it when he doesn't call me Abi like everyone else. "First, I do have friends, you just don't know them."

"Tape me, please," I huff out, holding out my palm as if he were a living tape dispenser.

"Second," he continues, ignoring my interruption with practiced ease, "I want to remind you that I am here; therefore, I obviously understand the concept of being a good friend."

His glare stares back at me for a long beat before finally slapping a piece of tape in my hands. "There, happy?"

"Thank you," I state without giving his speech a second thought as I smooth the piece of tape onto the edges of the welcome banner that keeps wobbling in the lazy Texas wind.

As I coax the banner's corners back into line, his deep, unamused voice punctuates the silence. "I'm just asking for everyone to have a smidge of common sense before dropping a small fortune on all of this."

"Okay, that's it." I turn to him slowly, unsure if his frustration is surface-level or a root to something much more profound. Calmly, I add, "Sometimes it's not about what makes sense or seems practical. Sometimes people just want... memories." I gesture vaguely to our surroundings, taking in the twinkling lights draped from the expansive oak trees and the wildflower centerpieces bobbing on linen-draped tables. His posture relaxes a little, and the tightness in his shoulders eases. His stare has lightened, not as angry, but more understanding.

"Now," I add, "let's both get presentable because, if I'm being honest, this sweaty version of you doesn't feel camera-ready." I'm not even sure I believe the lie I told him. Despite how much Chase and I take stabs at each other, I have always wondered if there was an underlying flirtatious tone on his part. I know that I have attempted to bridge that gap over the years, but his mixed signals give me no indication of how he really feels. In all intents and purposes, Chase is gorgeous; his ruggedness is something that many women dream about. Seeing him like this - annoyed, but loyal enough to his friends that he will show up when he thinks it is unnecessary - makes him even more attractive to me. "Oh, be ready for photos at 4:30," I toss over my shoulder as I walk away, determined not to see his reaction – afraid that if I did, my own desire might win this battle between desire and annoyance.

I rush to help Macy prepare for her and Luke's renewal of vows. Inside, the air is perfumed with Macy's favorite jasmine lotion, blending with the faint tang of lemon polish on the hardwood floors.

Macy and her mom work over silk ribbons and pearl hairpins, their laughter fluttering like songbirds around the room. Macy's cheeks glow with excitement as she smooths the folds of her ivory chiffon gown. My mind keeps drifting to the moment when I get to walk arm-in-arm with Chase down the aisle. Almost as if Macy knows I have a thing for Chase, she created a maid-of-honor and best man dance later tonight. When she told me about her "brilliant" idea, there was a small twinkle in her eye as if she was up to something. I've been able to dodge her questions over the last year, terrified she would tell Luke about my mild-ish crush on Chase, and it would somehow be relayed to him. His constant snarky comments and closed-off demeanor are my never-ending reminder that I'm an annoyance - and frankly, if he wants to keep up that grumpy façade, I'll play along.

"Abs," Macy singsongs from across the room, "did Chase show up?" I remind myself that my face cannot give away how difficult he has been all day. The last thing I want is for Macy to be stressed that Chase will cause problems. "Yes, he is out there somewhere." My voice strains as I push my annoyance through each word, praying it throws her off.

"But did he look handsome?" Her words surprise me, taking me off guard just enough that my chilly look feels warmer than I would like.

"I'm not sure what you consider handsome," I groan. "But if you want to know if he is wearing a pre-determined outfit and is great at handing me pieces of tape after I threaten his life." My shrug feels half-hearted under the weight of her glare.

Macy's giggles send a sense of gloom down my spine. I know that she knows I am holding my true feelings to my chest. "Well, I still think you should give him a chance. Y'all would be so cute together," she tries to emphasize each of her words, and all it does is annoy me more. I am once again reminded that we do not see Chase in the same light. I see him as grumpy, and she sees him as a teddy bear you just have to get to know.

"And I still think that you aren't reading the situation properly. He hates me. He annoys me. That's all there is to talk about." When I look her in the eyes, I sigh, giving her a warning that I don't want to have this discussion again.

"Fine, but eventually I will make you both see how stupid you are being over this." Oh, the things I wish I could tell her, how yes, he annoys me, but he feeds a flame deep inside me even more.

I push everything aside as I work diligently on the final touches and get Macy down the aisle in time.

But tonight, after all of my maid-of-honor duties have expired, I will take in this day and allow myself to have fun. And as the string lights twinkle overhead and hordes of laughter surround us, I'll pretend Macy's orchestrated dance between Chase and me is something that he wanted to do and not forced to do.

Chapter Four

CHASE

"**W**elp, **we did** our part, didn't we?" Abigail's soft, sweet voice floats through the hush of the ceremony space, soft and lilting like the curl of smoke from a candle. As we reach the end of the wedding aisle, she loosens her arm around mine. We step onto the final plank of polished wood, its surface warm from the beating late-afternoon sun, as she slips her arm free. The slide of her skin against my cotton shirt sends sparks crackling up my spine. I stiffen, cursing my own stubborn resolve when my mind wanders to our first meeting and how she stole my breath and made the room light up around her the moment she stepped into it. I swore I would keep my distance, but her joy has been my undoing since day one.

I've allowed only polite hellos and greetings when around her, only giving myself permission to consider her as merely an acquaintance. Macy has asked me several times if I have a thing for Abigail, but I have successfully pushed the topic off. If Macy, or anyone else, really knew that I have been thinking about Abigail as anything more than a passing ship in the night, I would never hear the end of it. Scenes of Abigail in my kitchen - blonde curls flowing down her back, flour smudged on her cheeks - as she and Charlie press cookie dough into shapes often sweep into my mind. Such a simple but loving task that I want in my life. She's the sort of woman who winds your world around her finger, while I'm the kind of man who can't promise a future. My life is too messy for certainty, and she deserves a steady, comforting love that reminds her how perfect she is.

A sharp snapping of her petite fingers yanks me back. Abigail's cool, unamused gaze stops me in my tracks, impatience dripping between each snap. "Earth to Chase," she demands while the distant murmur of wedding chatter and clinking champagne flutes keeps me distracted.

Heat floods my cheeks. "Um," I am more confused than I should be. I keep going back to remembering how her arm felt next to mine. That thought makes everything dissolve around me. "Sorry. What's up, Abigail?" My voice sounds loud in the sudden quiet. She tilts her head, golden spirals catching every strand of sunlight, and exhales an exaggerated breath. "Do you need anything from the groom's changing room? I'm headed that way, but I guess that's the thanks I get for offering." Her tone is light, but I see the flicker of hurt and disappointment in her eyes.

I swallow, hoping the wasted second will slow my racing heart. "No, I'm good. Thanks, though." She turns, the silk of her dress whispering over her legs, and I want to trail after her, tug that fabric off every curve in private and lose myself in the dips of her waist - my mind races, sketching the secrets hidden beneath her gown.

"Dad! Daaad!" Charlie's voice slices through my tangled thoughts as she looks up to me with her bright, insistent eyes, untouched by my inner storm. Charlotte, or Charlie as I call her, is full of sass and determination as she tugs on my sleeve. Her red-buffed cheeks and freckles gleam in the sun as she points across the expansive plot of land beyond the seating area. She may only be nine years old, but she already has the attitude of a teenager.

She is my greatest joy, but the cause of my biggest headaches. When she and I left her mom's house, I had no idea what I was doing. I just knew that she deserved more than the mom who didn't care about her. Once I realized I had to leave and take Charlie with me, I called Bell, my little sister, and we ran. Landing in Pigeon Lake was not where I thought we would go, but when I got my oil rig job, the pay was too good to turn down. Bell stepped up to help with the day-to-day tasks with Charlie while I kept us fed.

I kneel to her level. "Yes, Charlie?" We have been working on manners and interrupting people, but I don't think I can lecture her about interrupting my daydreaming.

She lifts her eyebrows, eyes shining bright. "Can I go with Ryder to the creek over there?" I follow her fingers to the narrow ribbon of water that winds through the Hamilton's' property, separating their land from Luke's plot of land.

"I don't think you should. What if something happens? I can't go to watch out for you," I say, hoping I sound lighter than I feel right now.

Ryder, who is eleven and already quick as a whip, pipes up from Charlie's other side. "No, sir, there is hardly any water left in it. We are in a drought - did you forget?" Ryder's squeaky voice responds. As I look down at the boy, I say a quick prayer that he won't be a bigger issue when he and Charlie get older and hormones start racing. They have been friends for years, but when do friends become more than friends?

"Yes, Ryder - I understand that - but someone has to keep her safe," I grunt, trying not to roll my eyes at the kid. It isn't his fault.

"I can keep her safe, Sir. I once grabbed a snake as it slithered towards my mom. So, I'm tough." He puffs out his chest as if he wrestled a grizzly bear.

"Ryder," I retort, "it was a tiny garter snake. Your little sister could have taken care of that thing." Ryder's jaw tightens, but he's not truly offended.

I run my fingers through my short hair, looking around to see if there are any other kids that I could send with them. I would even settle for a rogue aunt or neighbor.

When I can't find anyone to go with them, I shake my head in defeat. "Fine, you can go. But if you see a single snake, of any kind," I stress while I side-eye Ryder, "it better be taken care of."

Both kids nod in unison, relief washing over their faces. They both start running towards the creek, Charlie's dress blowing in the wind while Ryder's boots kick up dirt as he chases after her. "Stand down, big brother." My sister's light voice scares me out of my trance, filled with worry.

I glance over to my sister with a death glare. "Stand down? Nope. If I had listened to you every time you told me to 'stand down' when you were going out on dates, who knows where you would have ended up." My hands find my waist as I stand tall over Bell.

Bell's lips curve into a razor-sharp smile. "And you never believed me when I said Hayes was just my friend."

I narrow my eyes at her, blinded by the beautiful Texas sunset. "And I stand by that he's too old for you, and you two have nothing in common," I grunt, replaying every time I saw Hayes, one of my longest friends, give Bell googly eyes. I know he has been plotting how he would be able to snatch her to keep for decades, and I'll be damned if I ever let that happen.

Bell lets out an exasperated tut. "You're pricklier than ever, aren't you? Does it come naturally, or have you had to practice it?" I can hear the humor in Bell's voice, but I refuse to look at her. My eyes have returned to Charlie as I see her and Ryder have made it to the creek.

Without another word, I pivot and stalk across the linen-draped tables towards Luke's makeshift bar, which he created for their wedding... or second wedding... or whatever in the hell this event has been. The bar consists of a battered plank of wood lying flat over two large, round tree trunks where Lucas etched their initials. The sweet scent of jasmine vine drifts on the humid night air, while distant laughter shakes the strings of lights overhead. My throat is sandpaper dry as I grab a beer like a drowning man needing a lifeline.

Bell's voice drifts after me. "You'd better hurry, Abi is over there. I hear she is scouting for a dance partner." Her voice is too loud as I start looking around for evidence that anyone overheard her wisecracks. She has always suspected I was secretly pining for Abi, but I have always denied everything.

My chest tightens into a vise as I take in the clusters of gossiping guests while their voices rise like cicadas in the darkness. I press my palm into the dark wood of the bar, fighting through the pricks of splinters biting through my skin. I finish the last sip of my beer before I reach for another frosty amber bottle beading with condensation.

Before I can turn, Abigail materializes at my elbow, light as a breeze through the pines, head cocked like she is reading my mind. "Did Bell just say something to you about me?" Her green eyes, fringed with thick lashes, lock into mine.

I force a casual shrug in response. "Nope," I say, giving an extra emphasis on the popping of the p. I'm hoping my tired shake of my head helps to sell my response.

"Why are you lying to me?" Abigail quips, fully facing towards me now and leaning on the bar. Her response confirms that my response didn't, indeed, sell my denial.

My chest hollows, every word tastes like grit. "What do you want, Abigail? Haven't you chastised and annoyed me enough today?" I continue my gaze forward, worried I would let my eyes slide over her tight dress too much.

Her grin is a blend of sugar and steel. "I don't think I will ever meet my quota in annoying you. It's my superpower." The smile in her voice is potent as she continues. "But I also need you to take me home tonight. Mace picked me up for our hair appointment this morning, so I don't have a vehicle. Do you mind?"

Fuck. My gut tightens into a knot as I remind myself I need distance from her, not be in tighter vicinities. "There has to be someone else who could take you home. What about Lyla Franks? She lives like two doors down from you. She would be perfect." I blurt, but it comes out too harshly.

"Ah, well, I already asked Lyla, but she is staying with Rosie Helms. Rosie Helms lives in the opposite direction from my house." Her voice is light, teasing, but those steady eyes pin me in place. That feels rude to ask of them, don't you think?" Abigail's smart ass comments grate on me, but only because I want nothing more than to get the opportunity to watch

Abigail walk away from me, the image of her silhouette slipping away in the headlights as she shuts her front door.

"There are a hundred other people here, Abigail. You could ask them." I push, hoping she drops the subject.

Her laugh sounds like a chime of church bells in the night. "Perfect! Thanks, Chase." Abigail yells over her shoulder as she walks away from me, leaving me standing in awe, holding my beer and wishing for someone to save me.

I watch as she vanishes in the throng of people while the cool night presses in around me. I wonder if she's stealing my time - when all I've ever wanted is to steal hers.

Chapter Five

CHASE

"**She's getting too** big for me to do this," I grumble, the engine idling as I ease the latch and lower my daughter into the truck's backseat. She's still clinching the wedding bouquet as I slip her seatbelt on. The night air is cool and fragrant with pine as it wafts in through the open windows. It pains me to know that Charlie will soon not be small enough for me to take care of, that she will soon not need me anymore, and I don't know if I'm ready for that.

The passenger-side door creaks open, and Abigail's boots click against the metal running board as she climbs in. She eases herself onto the fabric seat with practiced grace and closes the door so gently it barely nudges its frame. My fingers tighten around the steering wheel as she gently closes the door, the same careful way she helped Charlie with her wedding shoes earlier. My heart twists at the contrast: this feisty, smart-mouth woman who has given me hell all day can snap into a delicate flower, her kindness concealed under her layers of sass. Beneath her armor, she dances around others in a way to make sure they are happy and comfortable.

In the pale glow of the dashboard, Abigail sits with her one leg crossed over the other, her long curls coiling around her fingers in a nervous spiral. The soft rustling of her hair against the headrest seems impossibly loud in the quiet cab. My eyes slip in the rearview mirror, taking a quick glance at Charlie to make sure she is still asleep.

"Why are you so quiet?" I murmur, turning the key. "Are you nervous?" I ask, wondering if I'm saying too much. I can't help but push as my tires meet the dirt road that leaves a path of dust in our wake. "This isn't the first time you have sat in my passenger seat, Abigail. I know when you are lying."

She huffs, turning to stare out the window at the expansive darkness. It's as if that darkness holds some secret she'd rather keep to herself. "Don't be annoying, Chase. Just drive me home so I can peel these heels off and be out of this dress."

I swallow through a lump in my throat, thinking of her feet tapping on my dashboard earlier, polished toes scuffing the plastic. That feels like my version of heaven. "You could, uh, take your heels off now if you need to," I say before my tongue can catch up with my thoughts.

She shoots me a sideways glance, eyes bright in the dash light, then bends her knees and slips each slender foot out of her strappy shoes. The soft click of the heels hitting the rubber mat makes me worry - what if all the dust and gravel I have tracked in will stain her shoes or dress? But she doesn't seem to care; she tucks her feet beneath her like she's done it a hundred times before, making herself at home in a space where no woman has belonged since Anna left. The realization hits me harder than the potholes we're driving over.

"Do you mind if I roll the window down, or do you think it will wake up Charlie?" Abigail's whispers as she turns to glance behind us at my daughter. Her thoughtfulness makes me want to reach out and grab her hand.

"I think it will be fine. She is used to it," I reply, pressing the button to draw down the windows. The glass descends, and a rush of night air - laden with crickets and distant pasture scents - swirls in. George Strait's mellow twang pumps out of the speakers. I take in the situation, enjoying riding next to the woman of my dreams, letting her smile trick me into thinking she is mine.

Between her low hums along with the music, Abigail tries to make small talk with me by asking easy questions such as whether I like my job, how Charlie is doing in school, and how Bell's veterinary clinic is doing. These are all easy answers, but they are nothing that I want to talk about. I want to talk about her. I want to know why someone who can read off literature with military precision also rides in my truck with her bare feet on my dashboard. I want to understand how the woman who argued with me about tape for twenty minutes can now sit quietly beside me, humming George Strait under her breath like she's forgotten I'm here.

I continue driving circles around the mile-long sections of road, wasting time while watching Abigail lean into the wind, hair whipping free of its coils as she sings old country songs into the warm night. One of her curls falls into her eyes, and without thinking, my hand reaches up and pulls the hair out of her face. Time stops as she completely freezes, no longer waving her hand out the window. Before I fully register what I have done, Abigail turns to look at me, shock written across her face. We have never touched more than a quick dance at Meryl's. Touching her like this, in the darkness of the country roads, feels much more intimate. It is too intimate for our relationship. We bicker; we don't show our gentle sides to each other.

"Why did you do that?" She whispers. The question trembles with vulnerability I've never seen before.

I grip the steering wheel, knuckles white, all the words I've wanted to say slam into my chest. But all that comes out is, "I, uh, sorry." I'm too afraid to look at her, scared I'll crack under her glare. I have given myself a firm order: don't be gentle with her and keep my walls up, but the glow of my dashboard makes that problematic.

She's quiet for a heartbeat, then says, almost defensively, "I would've done it myself eventually, you know?"

My eyes roll as I grip the steering wheel tighter. "I know that, Abigail. I said I'm sorry." The lie tastes bitter. What I want to say is that I've watched those curls catch in her lashes at Meryl's, at Lucas's barbecues, at the library when she thinks no one's looking, and every damn time, my fingers have itched to do precisely what I just did.

Her eyes never leave my portrait, still staring me down like I am about to say something else. "You've been giving me that same scowl since I first met you? You don't have to be so... stand-offish, you know?" Her voice cuts through me like a paring knife.

"Who said I'm grumpy?" I snap, immediately feeling the words are too sharp. "Why are you always so happy?"

"Who said I was happy?" She responds, catching me off guard with her words. I've never imagined her anything but sunshine and laughter.

Before I can answer, the gravel drive to her house crunches under my tires, despite taking the long way to her home. All I wanted was extra time in her presence, but once I made the situation uncomfortable, something tells me I may have lingered too long. As I put the truck in park, my eyes find Charlie, still curled up in the backseat, fast asleep.

Abigail peels off her seatbelt before grabbing her heels, not taking time to put them back on. Opting, instead, to walk barefoot across her yard. I wait until I see her open the front door and make it inside. I allow myself to pause for three more seconds until I see her lights flip on.

"Real smooth, Dad, real smooth," Charlie's sleepy voice makes me jump. I clear my throat, the ache in my chest deepening. Tonight, I convinced myself I was just driving her home. But as I shift into reverse, I know it wasn't just about the road. It was about Abigail and a moment I'll replay for a long time to come.

Chapter Six

ABIGAIL

The soft thrum of little sneakers on the well-worn wooden floors echoes through the low shelves, punctuated by bursts of whispered giggles so fierce they might as well be shouts. I stand behind the circulation desk, my heart pounding with the same energy these children exude. My hair is tucked neatly behind my ears while I wear my favorite cardigan. I'm always hoping the look gives "cool librarian" vibes. After all, the last librarian here, Miss Arnett, was the very definition of forbidding. A shriveled old woman who would sneer at anyone who didn't love Jane Austen. I can still hear her acid-etched voice banishing modern stories and asking questions like, "What's the point of reading if you read anything other than the classics?" I swear she hid a tape of her saying that in the air ducts or something, because I can still hear that old hag saying it like a ghost scripting cruel literary mandates through the vents.

A small hand tugs at my wrist, and a squeaky voice interrupts my daydreaming. "Misssss Klinnnne... Hello?" Ryder's dark eyes stare up at me, his tiny fingers wiggling around my skin.

"Hi Ryder, how are you today?" I ask, trying to ground myself back to where I'm not plotting how I can continue to be seen as cool.

His lips press into an annoyance. "Wondering when we are starting science hour," Ryder responds, obviously irked with my absence, "you're running four minutes late." His dramatic glance at his watch is ridiculously cute as the plastic strap squeaks as he gestures.

A laugh escapes me as mock shock and horror fill my face. "Oh yes! Isn't today Albert Einstein Day?" I ask as if I have no idea and didn't plan the entire month's calendar. Something about kids, they always want to feel as if they are keeping us all together and get to repeat the schedule back at you.

"Yep, so can we start?" Wow, this kid is needy. Despite how much I want to put him off just because he needs to learn patience, I know he is correct, and I should get started. Before I get another dramatic check of his watch, I pull out the few props I'm planning to use to better understand Einstein and his grand contributions to our lives.

Before I can savor the drama of my own show, a firm voice behind Ryder cuts through the air. "You don't have to be a jerk, Ryder. Can't you see Abi is busy?"

I turn to find Charlie planted firmly behind him, her arms crossed, and her chin tipped upward in perfect imitation of every indignant adult she's ever seen. The sun slants through the tall library windows onto her auburn hair, giving her an almost haloed edge.

Ryder's mouth twists in petulance. "Charlie, my mom says you should always call your elders Miss or Mrs or Sir. So, you should have said Miss Kline." He smirks as though he's just delivered the final word. Elder? Who does this kid think he is? I just decided to take my time starting our science experiment today.

Charlie narrows her eyes. "I'm allowed to call her Abi because she's my dad's friend, which makes her my friend. I don't think you can say that, can you?" Her tone is just as condescending as his was to her.

She turns her back to him, rolling her shoulders back like a football pro finishing a game against their rival, and stalks to the designated kids' area. Ryder's jaw falls open, and I can't help but grin behind my mask of librarian propriety.

"Okay, everyone," I say, raising my voice just enough to gather their attention. Some of them are looking at the props I sat out while others are sitting cross-legged on the floor, waiting patiently for me to start. "Time to talk about Einstein!"

"We're not friends, Charlie," murmurs Chase as we walk by, finally making his presence known.

Charlie is feeling extra feisty today as she stabs back at her dad. "You give her rides home sometimes. Would you do that to someone you didn't like?" His daughter stabs back, making Chase and me make eye contact, fear written all over our faces.

Chase squirms under Charlie's glare. "Sometimes we have to choose to be nice to people, even when we don't want to." Their stare-down continues as Ryder and I watch the match like a game of tennis. "Kind of like you should do with Ryder."

Even at nine years old, Charlie already has her eye-rolling game down, which she shows off to her dad as she spins away from us. "Totally not worth it, Dad."

Chase shows me where she learned how to roll her eyes after I call Chase "friend" as I take a seat in front of the dozen or so kids.

A hush falls over the group as chalk-white goggles slip onto curious faces, and the library's usual hush feels electric. An hour passes in a whirl of childlike questions and the soft whine of the vent, the thud of small chairs, and the hiss of experiments all swirl into the perfect harmony of discovery.

This is one of the many ideas I came up with when I started working at the library. Miss Arnett kept everything so stuffy and didn't allow kids to explore, question, or even talk with each other while they took in everything we offered. Once she passed, I knew I wanted to overhaul the whole thing. Growing up, the library was the one place I felt safe and could hide from the world. I wanted to create that for other kids by catering to their needs and interests. Initially, the science projects were just a way to get the kids involved, but they quickly took off, and now we have a waiting list for each month. If this is the legacy I provide the kids, then I did my part.

As I finish placing the last pieces of equipment into my box, I feel a shift in the atmosphere, and I glance up. When I do, I see Chase glaring at me, looking annoyed, but sexy as hell.

"What's up, Chase?" I try to sound annoyed, but I'm sure I failed.

He is leaning against the circulation desk, arms crossed over his broad chest. His blonde hair brushes his collar while his usually short facial hair appears to be a little more grown out than usual. "Abigail." Chase flatly says, making me feel as if I am the one who requested his presence. Even his use of my full name feels loaded with intent. "Charlie wanted me to ask if you'd join us for dinner. I'm sure you have better things to do, but she forced me to come ask."

Charlie appears beside him, leaning forward with her elbows on the desk and eyebrows dancing in a silent plea. The halo of sunlight makes her look like our Goddess of Mischief. I swallow against the sudden dryness in my throat.

"Why?" I ask, folding my arms and buying myself time to come up with a good reason not to go with them.

Chase shrugs, muscles shifting beneath his shirt. "Beats me, but she said that since we are friends, it's rude not to ask. We are going anyway, so if you want to join us, then fine. If not, I will tell her you can't, and we can drop it."

"Please, Abi, I will try to make Dad act nice to you." Charlie's pleas are endearing, and the reason why I can't help but say yes.

In defeat, I release a breath, sighing to show my pretend irritation with him. "Fine, where are we going?"

"Not sure yet. Jump in my truck, and we will go wherever Miss Nosey over there wants. She is usually in charge. I can bring you back to your car afterward." His strong hands sliding through his facial hair do things to me that I don't want to think about right now.

"Okay, let's go." Charlie squeaks as she realizes I agreed to this. The late-afternoon light follows us outside, and when his fingers accidentally brush mine, a heat spreads through my ribs. This should be a sign that I'm too deep into feelings with this.

Chapter Seven

CHASE

How in the world did I get myself into this? I'm perched on a wrought-iron chair at the edge of the Mexican restaurant's patio, squinting against the late-afternoon sun. Across the little mosaic-topped table, Abigail and Charlie exchange whispered jabs every time I lift a fork or clear my throat. The air is thick with the scent of grilled chilies and cilantro, the clatter of dishware, and the gentle hum of cicadas in the nearby oaks. My shirt's already damp with sweat, and I haven't even finished my first beer.

I slide a few bills onto the dark wood table that includes one of Lucas' signature circles in it, while the coins ring against the metal check holder. My chair scrapes the flagstones as I push back, sending a jolt of noise throughout the courtyard. All at once, diners look up, eyebrows raised, just in time to catch Abigail and Charlie collapsing into giggles at my expense. I never asked for this comedy duo tagging along.

If you'd asked me before tonight, I'd have told you I wanted peace and quiet - just me, a plate of enchiladas, and a cold beer. But this? Watching Abigail's easy laugh scattering like sunlight? I realize that's not what I want at all. Her bright energy is infectious, seeming to pull everyone into her orbit, breathing life into the simplest moment. Despite my protests, even I'm able to admit that I haven't laughed more in a very long time.

Charlie pops open the passenger door. "Hey Abi," she calls, "how do you feel about going on a drive with us?"

Abigail glances at me - those green eyes huge and uncertain, begging me to nod her free. I lift a hand. "I'm sure she has something else she needs to do tonight."

This is my failed attempt to give Abigail an escape plan, but Charlie isn't buying it. "What do you have to do tonight, Abs?" Charlie prods, refusing to let the subject go.

"Nothing fun," she pauses, biting her lip while still trying to make out what my facial expressions are. "I guess we can go for a drive. Only if I pick the music, though." This causes me to groan because, knowing Abigail, she is about to put on Taylor Swift or something.

I catch her smirk as she plugs her phone into the dash. Both girls roll down their windows as I turn off on the nearest dirt road. I follow suit and allow the warm breeze to whip across my face as I pick up speed. When "Carry On" by Pat Green crackles through the speakers, I grin without thinking, letting the chorus fill the cab.

Golden light filters through the oak trees, lining our path, and the dirt beneath the tires kicks up little puffs of red dust. We pass miles and miles of wild sunflowers, lining both sides of the two-lane road, reminding us how simple and beautiful our world can be. Abigail's hands are waving in the sunshine, wind is whipping around Charlie's hair, and I start daydreaming about this being an every-night thing. The mention of Hill Country, Texas, reminds me of my childhood, chasing girls, and keeping my sister, Bell, out of trouble. Nobody has seen a beautiful country until they have been to Hill Country, and that's something I would die on.

Abigail's hands dance above her head, fingers strumming invisible guitar strings while Charlie's head bounces to a fiddle solo only real fans would be able to replicate. For a moment, nothing exists but that song and the three of us - carefree and alive.

Abruptly, Abigail falls silent. I glance sideways - her mouth hangs open, pupils dilated, as if she's seeing me for the first time.

My heart stutters. "What's up, Abigail? You look like you've spotted a ghost.

She blinks rapidly, sarcasm dripping from her words, "I didn't know you could smile. I'm in shock. Am I dreaming or something?" Without thinking, I slide my fingers under her chin and gently close her mouth. Her skin is warm, and her lips are soft.

"Ha ha," I say, clearing my throat. "You're hilarious." I turn my gaze back to the road, chasing away any thoughts that shouldn't be there. But the image of her startled face - her full lips parted - will visit me in the dark for nights to come.

The sun dips lower, painting the sky in bruised purples and oranges. Crickets begin their evening chorus as the red dirt ribbon stretches out before us, awaiting the next turn. And for now, that's enough.

Chapter Eight

ABIGAIL

Dusk settles over the landscape as Chase steers the pickup around a bend, gravel popping beneath the tires. A cloud of dust rises in our headlights when another vehicle approaches and stops alongside us. Windows whir down in unison - Charlie's practically bouncing in her seat while Chase's jaw tightens. He answers his friend with clipped responses, clearly trying to end the roadside chat, when Lizzy, Charlie's friend, leans across from the passenger seat, pleading for Charlie to spend the night. My stomach knots instantly. These one-on-one evening drives with Chase require mental armor I haven't had time to put on today, and now I might face him alone, without Charlie's chatter to fill the silence between us.

With a resigned nod, Chase gives his permission. Charlie squeals, already halfway out of the truck before he can change his mind, her sneakers crunching against the gravel as she races toward Lizzy. As taillights disappear around the bend, Chase turns to face me, his expression caught between a scowl and something softer - lips pressed tight, but eyes betraying a flicker of something that makes my pulse skip.

The cab is bathed in the soft, amber glow of the radio's display, its needle dancing across the dial as it pours '90s country into the night air. The engine hums beneath us, mingling the distant chorus of cicadas and the faint rustle of mesquite leaves in the warm Texas breeze. These Saturday-night drives have become our ritual. Sometimes we pause at the diner outside of town, but other times we pack a picnic to eat later. No matter what the plan is, I soak up every moment I can. Without Charlie here, it feels much different suddenly.

I've made one colossal miscalculation: what began as a harmless crush on Chase has blossomed into something much, much greater. Sharing these meaningless moments with him and Charlie has only made my feelings grow even greater. I would never confess this to anyone - not even Macy- but I have gone beyond a crush and landed with real, unmanageable feelings for him.

A few bars of "Strawberry Wine" by Deana Carter float from the speakers. I catch Chase's fingers flinching toward the volume knob, knowing it is my favorite song from this era. The notion causes a small smile to tug at my lips. He'll never admit how keenly he catalogs my quirks and those little things that make me happy, but he almost always does these little things that reveal he's paying attention.

But let's be honest, I do the same for him. I grab an extra slice of Redbird's triple-chocolate cake whenever I know he's had a rough day, offering it with a conspiratorial grin. He's started to flash me that rare, genuine smile when I hand it over - a small victory in our unspoken war of tenderness.

I'm lost in these reflections when the truck slows to a stop and the red dust swirling behind us settles. Moonlight spills across the hood. "What's wrong?" I ask, confused about why he's stopping. We've pulled off here before, but tonight feels charged like the air before a thunderstorm.

Without saying a word, Chase opens his door and quietly steps out. The heated look in his eye when he stares back at me before shutting the door sends a shiver up my back. If this were an '80s John Hughes movie, I'd be sure he was about to sweep me into a dramatic kiss. Instead, I briefly entertain the darker thought that this may be when and where he kills me.

The passenger-side door quietly opens, bringing me back to reality. The dilemma of 'murder or '80s movie? Murder or an '80s movie?' Plays over and over in my mind as Chase lifts his palm up, reaching out towards me, and the flick of his finger, inviting me to join him, whirls me back to the present.

His deep, groveling voice fills the silence and anxiety surrounding me. "Why do you look like I'm about to kill you?"

"Is this when you kill me?" I force a laugh, hoping he takes it as a joke. "We're pretty far from help, but I'm sure my scream would echo to town."

His blank face tells me how annoyed he is with my questions. "If I were going to kill you, I'd have done it years ago, just to save me the trouble of listening to you." His deep sigh sends heat shooting through me. "Now, use my hand and get out. We need to talk."

I consider scolding him for that tone, but there's something about it that makes my pulse quicken. Swallowing, I let him guide my hand into his rough palm - calloused from fieldwork and rig days - while mine are soft from library story hours, which feels startlingly delicate by comparison.

I assumed he would let go of my hand as soon as my feet were planted on the ground, but the moment I try to retrieve it from his firm grip, he tightens, denying my ability to dissolve our physical touch. He leads me around to the tailgate, then hesitantly lets go of my hand so he can flip the tailgate open. A shiver arcs down his spine at that moment - or maybe that's my imagination.

He wraps both of his rough hands around my waist and sits me on the cool metal so gently, it's like he sees me as a delicate egg.

I shift, and he doesn't step back as expected. Without thinking, my legs widen, allowing him to stand too close. His unique scent of earth and sweat envelops me. His hands slip into his Wrangler pockets, thumbs hooked, while he stares at the ground.

"Thank you for taking Charlie under your wing lately," he blurts, gaze fixed on a patch of dirt at his feet. His voice is rougher than usual, taut with emotions he's trying to rein in. "You don't have to do that, but having another strong woman in her life means a lot to me."

I reach out, brushing stray hair from his temple. "Chase, you don't have to thank me for showing up for you or Charlie. I love that little spitfire of yours. It isn't a chore to be around her; she provides me with the same amount of joy. If you ever need anything, please let me know." The ache I see in his shoulders makes my chest tighten. What ghosts are haunting him to make him so sad?

He glances up, eyes dark. "She really looks up to you, you know? That's not really fair that you have to take on that pressure, but that girl trusts you. I'm..." He clears his throat, lips parting and closing as he searches for the right words. "... just glad she has someone like that. You know, other than me and Bell."

"She is like a mini-me, despite your best efforts to stop that." His eyes shoot back at me, not catching the jovial tone I was trying to lead with. I give him a playful nudge, but he only softens enough to unfold his arms.

His hands drag through his hair as he looks at the setting sun over the far hills. "She really is perfect, isn't she? I hate that she is getting older and doesn't want to hear how much I love her."

"Give her a few years, and she will be back loving you quicker than you think." I try, but miss his leg as I kick playfully, but he only smirks for the tiniest of seconds. "But serious question," I say.

This makes him perk up, fearing what I may ask him. "How can you love her so much and be so passionate about hating me when we are the exact same person?" I am clearly joking, but could I be digging for a little bit of warmth back? Absolutely.

We constantly have this dance where I'm nice to him, he seems grumpy about it, he continues to do the tiniest, nicest thing back, and then I try to keep it going, and he shuts down.

"I don't hate you, Abigail," he says before I can answer, voice flat but eyes softened. "Why would you think that?" If it weren't for the deep creases between his eyebrows, I would think he was joking.

"Oh, I don't know." I shrug, heart fluttering out of my chest. "Maybe it is your perpetual scowl and sarcasm? But I choose to look past that." My teasing falls flat as I watch the tension return between his brows. His deep stare forces me to look out towards the field of bluebonnets swaying in the light Texas breeze.

He inhales sharply. "I stopped hating you a while ago, Abigail." His words are almost a whisper as he steps closer, shrinking the space between us to nothing. "Do you want me to hate you?"

My throat goes dry. The tailgate metal presses against my calves; his hands lean beside me, bracketing me in his silent gravity. It's like all my words have escaped me, and I'm unable to speak as I calculate how little space there now is between me and the man I have entirely fallen for. The fire in his eyes is running laps over my features as he takes me in. Since words still can't come to me, I meekly shake my head, communicating that the last thing I want him to do is hate me. The deep swallow of his throat tells me I gave him the correct answer.

The pressure of his inspection causes me to break, desperate to change the subject to anything other than the situation we are in now. "What's that mean?" I quietly ask as my finger traces the branches of a tree that lines his arm. It sticks out because while two branches are full of foliage, the other branches are bare.

He growls, the sound vibrating through his chest. "Don't change the subject." His gaze drops to mine, fierce and demanding. Electricity crackles in his glance, and I know there's no turning back.

Chapter Nine

CHASE

've never seen Abigail look afraid of anything - her steady composure is legendary - but tonight her eyes are wide, her breathing shallow, and tremors quiver along her jaw. If I weren't pressed so close, feeling the heat radiating from under her skin under the moonlight, I'd swear she'd bolt. Over the last few months, I've learned every flicker of her expression, studying her like a class in school. Her fear now comes out from my words but from what I'm about to do. We both understand that this next moment will shape everything that comes after.

My heart hammers against my ribs. Hell, I'm scared shitless too - but losing her beside me, driving down countless dusty roads in my old pickup, is a terror far worse than any I know. I lean closer, my voice barely above the twitching breeze. "I'm going to kiss you now. Is that okay?"

Time fractures. The distant hum of crickets and the low rumble of my truck's engine fade into silence. I haven't risked my heart like this in ten years - not since Anna, Charlie's mom - slid out of my life. My lips, my time, my everything has been locked away, my longing buried under work and routine, until Abigail.

After seeing Abigail around Charlie and how much Charlie looks up to her, I have started to soften the stone walls around my heart and become more open to showing Abigail the softer side of me. Seeing her be firm when Charlie needed it, but also be there when Charlie's feelings were hurt, and it was a "girl thing," tore my heart apart.

Now, Abigail's thighs part further, telling me she's ready. I step forward, fingers weaving through the soft, silken curls at the nape of her neck. I pull her close and tilt her face upward until our lips meet.

The moment my lips touch hers, our entire future plays through my mind like an old movie. A movie I have owned for a long time, but kept on the shelf for safekeeping, not wanting to watch it in case I couldn't stop. A movie filled with worn leather seats, lazy sunsets, backyard barbeques, and small hands wrapped around ours - electricity arcs between us.

I press deeper, tasting the slight tang of her lipstick, the warmth of her breath. Her back arches, demanding I consume her more. I feel the curve of her body fitting into mine. My hands slide along the hem of her shirt, tracing the smooth arch of her spine. My mind wanders as I brace her hips and shift her closer to the edge of the tailgate. I need more of her. I am a starved man for the one person who can calm all my fear and apprehension.

A soft moaning slips from her, low and throaty. I'm helpless as the outline of my hardening cock presses into my jeans, every nerve ignited. She shifts, pelvis tilting, and I'm propelled into a world where nothing else exists but this fierce need and the plans I have for both of us.

I lift her effortlessly from the tailgate; her legs wrapped around my waist as her fingers tug my hair. She's telling me just how rough she'll let me be. I walk us towards the side of the truck, still aware that we can't be too loud or we will wake up my daughter, but that doesn't stop me from giving a couple of arbitrary thrusts into her core, making her moan louder and wrap me tighter in her grip.

I roam my hands over every inch of exposed skin - her collarbone warmed by perspiration, the soft slope of her shoulder. Each kiss melts more resistance from us both, until neither of us can tell where passion ends and fear begins. Suddenly, I hear a loud dog bark from across the field, which jerks me back to reality.

Guilt flares. As much as I dread it, I pull back from our kiss, walking us back to the dropped tailgate and gently placing Abigail back in her original location. We both lean back and take in the mess that I have caused for her. Abigail's hair is ragged, no longer in perfect spiral curls, but now with little whisps flying in the wind, and her lips are red from our kisses. She has never looked more beautiful under this Texas moon. I follow her gaze and quickly adjust myself, realizing I am giving away just how this woman makes me feel.

I straighten, brushing a thumb over her lower lip, surprised by how exposed I feel. "Sorry about that," I murmur, praying she isn't upset about what we just did. Surprisingly, a loud, boisterous laugh fills the night air, making my desire to lean back in spike.

Her laugh, rich and unguarded, peals in the darkness. "Don't you dare apologize for a kiss like that," she scolds, tugging at my shirt to bring me close to her. Her fingers find my belt loops, anchoring me to her. I tuck a strand of curls behind her ear as she continues. "I won't lie, I am slightly shocked that happened, but I'm not mad about it." A hush of peace settles around us.

Her long pause fills the empty space as I watch her brain move through all the questions or thoughts she may be coming up with. "I have to ask, though, what made you change your mind about me?" she asks, curious and half-teasing.

I rub the back of my neck, trying to find the words. "Honestly, when I saw you stick up for Charlie against those kids at the library last week, like she was your own and you were her scary Momma bear, I realized you were the one I had been looking for my whole life. Not many women would see Charlie as a prize to show off rather than a kid to hide because they aren't blood related."

She raises an eyebrow. "You got all of that from me shooing away that punk Rollins kid?" Her voice rises at the end, part question, part humor at the simplicity of the action.

"I mean, I always knew you were beautiful, but I'm not exactly the type of guy you would be with," I admit while her mind works overtime, wondering if she believes how simple my explanation really is.

"First, don't tell me the type of guy I should be with," she replies firmly, sighing and rolling her eyes at me. "Second, I'm glad you kissed me," she follows more softly that time.

Her bold grin is an invitation I can't resist. I lean in and brush my lips across hers. A low hum vibrates in her throat, and it feels like I'm coming home.

I pull back, heart clutching. "If I asked you on a date next weekend, would you go?" I pause, realizing how unfamiliar this is for me. My voice wavers in the uncertainty of my words. "Of course, that may not be something you want, and I definitely don't want to bring Charlie, or anyone really, into anything until we know what we are doing, but I would like to find out if we would work." I find myself rambling.

As if she can hear my fear, her soft hands squeeze mine, encouraging me to relax. "Of course I would. But I agree, we shouldn't tell anyone... not even Macy. No need to complicate things. Besides, I might decide I really do hate you."

"Yeah, you will absolutely decide you hate me," I joke. I bring her hands to my lips and place a few small, but lingering kisses across her knuckles.

"I think we need to head home before this gets too out of control. Deal?" I ask. Her nod is slight, but enough to tell me I made the right decision by leaving before it was too late.

I help her down from the tailgate and guide her to the passenger door. As she climbs in, I place a flirtatious tap on her firm ass and listen to her giggle as I shut the door. I put the truck back in drive, and in the glow of the dashboard, she stretches her hand across the console. I grasp it, thumb stroking her knuckles.

Tonight didn't go the way I thought it would, but hell, I think I'm excited for next weekend.

Chapter Ten

ABIGAIL

Chase slips into his truck parked in my driveway, the engine rumbling to life. I hadn't expected the confession, soft press of his lips, nor the playful smack on my ass, but I savored every second. My back leans against the cool, varnished wood of my front door, the grain pressing gently against my spine. My fingertips brush my trembling lips; I swear, I can still feel the faint warmth of his kiss - a whisper of tingles that danced across my skin.

This man, Chase, Mr. "What's the point of words when a grunt and an eyeroll suffice," Travers was not only unexpectedly tender, but also asked me on a date. I forced myself not to grin, though my heart was galloping like a stallion. After years of secret yearning, there was no way I could refuse.

My phone buzzes in my back pocket. I pray my rose-colored optimism would win out: maybe it was

Chase, unable to resist sending another stolen kiss. My realism scoffs as I know there is zero chance it is him. I flip my phone screen to life. The caller ID displays the wedding photo thumbnail of Macy and me, and the woman who has been hounding me for ages for gossip about whether I have a crush on Chase. What are the odds that she calls me the moment he rolls away?

"Damn! Did she see our kiss?" I whisper to the silent night, panic prickling up my spine. I'd promised Chase I'd keep our night's secret, no matter what. My potential happily-ever-after couldn't be derailed now. I hesitantly swipe to answer.

"Hey, Mace, what's up?" My voice emerges bright, but a tick of breathlessness betrays me.

"Abs? Are you okay?" Her concern crackles over the line, acute and knowing. Of course she heard something in my tone.

"Oh, yeah, of course. Sorry! I just got home." I force a laugh, reminding myself that I really can't control my voice. I annoy myself.

"Really? It's so late. I can't remember the last time I was able to stay out past 9:00 p.m." Her low chuckle makes me picture her curled under her duvet, Luke's hand massaging her feet in their nursery nook. "Anyways, memory lane is closed. What are you doing tomorrow?

"I've got a quick run into the library - book club stuff - then I'm free. Why?" I ask, knowing that Macy would never just call to ask me these types of questions without some idea already brewing.

"I was thinking about coffee at Redbird's around, say, nine? You in?"

I relax a little, realizing I may dodge any more prying tonight. "Yeah, I'm down."

"Perfect. So -" Her voice pauses, and my chest tightens. "Why were you out so late tonight? Any... special reason?" Ah, hell. Panic surges through me. Was she sitting outside my house, spyglass in hand? I reflexively yank my curtains aside to inspect the area around my house. The street lies empty in the moonlight - no Macy, no Lucas, no prying neighbor.

"Ha, no! I wish, though. Maybe next weekend," I retort, hoping that the line of questioning fades and I can continue to my pre-determined Hart of Dixie binge session.

"For some reason, I don't believe you, but we can talk more about this tomorrow. Love you, Abs. Night!" And with that, the line goes dead, and I release the breath I didn't realize I was holding.

***

The next morning, the bell above Redbird's door jingles as a wave of steamy Texas air pushes inside. We settle at a corner table beneath a fan humming like distant cicadas. Macy's purse thumps against the wooden surface, pulling me from my imaginary debate with an anti-opinion town elder and back to reality.

"Hey Abs, so sorry I'm late," she pants, smoothing the fabric of her maternity top over her belly. "I swear this kid hates me already. It hasn't even been born, and it's plotting my demise. What's there to hate when I'm delivering snacks and love?"

I raise my eyebrow. "I'm assuming that is a rhetorical question and not one that your easily wounded heart wants me to answer," I flatly reply, knowing her too well. After finding out she's pregnant, I have tried being nicer to her. Would she agree with that? Probably not.

She snorts. "Wow, someone didn't get laid after their date last night." Being friends for as long as we have means we both know not to take our words too harshly, but more to keep us both humble.

Not like I need anything to keep me humble about; I'm just a small-town librarian who hangs out with young kids or old ladies. In the non-creepy way, of course. Not much in between unless I go out with Macy and Bell on the weekends.

Macy, on the other hand, is about to release her first book, is having a baby, and has infamously returned to our hometown while still keeping her childhood sweetheart. Impostor syndrome plagues me almost every day. I want it all, but until last night, I've always been too afraid to take the steps to make it happen.

This isn't who I thought I would be when I graduated from college and moved back from Oklahoma. I wasn't in a sorority or anything like that, I'm not rich, after all, but I had such a good group of friends. With Macy hiding away up North, those were the friends that I clung to the most. But I never thought I would find myself being a watered-down version of myself.

"Ha ha, there was no date last night. Don't you think you would have been the first to know?" I ask, rolling my eyes in good faith of throwing Macy off the trail of my activities last night.

She pats her lap like a drum. "We need to fix that. I can't be popping out these kids and not having built-in best friends for them, ready to go. We need you married and pregnant." Her grin stretches wide, dimples deepening.

I poke at my latte absentmindedly. "You know," I pause, really taking in Macy's pregnancy glow, "I feel like those expectations may be too high for someone who has zero options on the horizon."

The words taste sour on my tongue. Saying Chase is a 'zero option' feels like I'm jinxing my own dreams. But Macy's eyebrow lift tells me she hears every implication.

Macy opens her mouth to retort my comment, but before she can, the chime over the door rings. I turn to see Chase and Charlie walking in. The moment Charlie sees me, she skips over to me and swings her arms around me.

My breath catches as I watch Chase's dusty boots cross the threshold. Upward, past rolled-up jeans and the crease of his faded work shirt, to the strong line of his jaw. He slips a hand into his pocket, the other brushing Charlie's braid. Then, catching my gaze, he winks. My cheeks flame hotter than the July sun outside.

Macy's voice brings me out of my daze as I hear her ask Chase what they are up to.

"Oh, Charlie wanted a cookie," Chase rumbles, voice gravelly with sleep. "Thought I'd grab a slice of their chocolate cake." His demeanor is more standoffish towards Macy, but he's clearly open whenever he risks a look at me.

At the mention of the cake, his glare rushes to meet mine, both knowing that this chocolate cake has been a point of conversation on our many night drives. "I guess it's a good thing I didn't buy all of it then, I considered it," I add, trying to change the subject to anything that would take that burning gaze away from me.

"Abs, you don't even like chocolate cake…" Macy quips with too much questioning in her tone.

"Oh, Abi gets it for my dad sometimes." Charlie pipes up, wide-eyed. "She never actually eats it herself.

My heart shutters. But before I can protest, Chase jumps in, making an effort to minimize his daughter's statement. "Only a couple of times, but I think it's just to prove she can be nice if she wants to. We all know how difficult that is for her." The annoyance in his voice is fake, but I catch the tiny squeeze of his fist whenever he looks my way - unspoken war between restraint and desire.

"Yeah, I don't think that's the case, Dad. Whatever you want to believe, though." Charlie rolls her eyes dramatically, making it clear she is done with this conversation. "Can I go say 'hi' to Ryder?" She barely gets out, her feet already leading her to her best friend.

"Considering you have already walked off, I guess that's okay," Chase says loudly, causing those around us to shoot their glances towards him.

Macy leans in, lowering her voice. "You know he's going to be a problem when they get older, don't you?"

Chase's jaw tightens. He bristles protectively as if the idea stings. "Like hell it will," Chase mutters as he makes his way to stand too close to Charlie.

"That man is going to have an aneurysm if he doesn't watch out." I declare as I turn my focus back to my friend.

The widest smile greets me as I look at my friend. "Yeah, I'm not sure if Ryder or your presence will be his demise." Macy shakes her head at me, making sure I understand that she is noticing the change in interactions between me and Chase.

"I'm not sure why I would be his demise. That man hates me." I respond, hoping that I sound more convincing and nonchalant than I feel.

"Oh yes, the man that was just standing here for sure hates you," sarcasm is laced deep in her words. "Only smiles when he sees you," she ticks one off her hand. "Been pretty eager to be our DD when we go to Meryl's on the weekends," ticking off a second finger. "Undressing you with his eyes while his daughter was standing next to him, and I'm here to witness it all," she says while she ticks finger three. "I can definitely see why you would think that." Macy looks smug as she leans back in her chair and rubs her swelling belly.

Before I can find a believable response, I feel a large, rough hand touch my shoulder, causing me to turn. Standing over me is the man who has been taking all of my thoughts for years now, the man I want to devour me like I'm his last meal. His hot breath spreads across my cheek as he leans down to whisper in my ear, "Don't worry about picking me up a cake tonight. I also got a piece of peach cobbler for you, Sunshine." My mouth is still hanging open in shock as he swings open the door of the coffee shop, and Macy's laugh fills the room.

Chapter Eleven

CHASE

'm not sure why that first kiss with Abigail Kline has turned me into someone else - a bolder, more brazen version of myself - but it has. My pulse thunders in my ears, my thoughts orbit around one person, one green-eyed girl. Tonight is our first real date, and I feel all the pressure I usually leave on the oil rigs roaring back tenfold. At work I wrestle with steel and hot pipes; but tonight, I have to wrestle with my own nerves, to deliver a type of date that Abigail deserves.

I crane my neck to glance at my reflection in the windshield as I pull the truck into her driveway. The cab still holds the faint tang of diesel and Charlie's old softball glove, but I straighten my button-down and smooth the front of my jeans. A quick check of the dashboard clock, I run my finger over the radio dial as "World on Fire" by Nate Smith starts crooning through the speakers. I hope this isn't a bad omen for our night ahead.

I hop out and give my freshly washed Chevy one more once-over. The moonlight pools on its hood like a spotlight on a stage. I clear my throat, then tap twice on Abigail's weathered wooden door. I wait. Twice more I rap, the soles of my boots shifting on the creaky porch planks. While I stand there, I take in her little front yard - barely a patch of grass compared to my few sprawling acres out by the old millpond. A chipped picket fence, a flowerbed where half the blooms are brown and brittle, and a cheeky sign staked between them reading "Where Plants Go to Die," complete with a miniature tombstone. I can't help but grin.

My mind starts wandering - if things go well tonight, would Abigail trade this in-town cottage for my quiet farmhouse? I shake my head as I tell myself I am getting way too far ahead of myself.

Just as I start second-guessing that I was supposed to pick her up, the door swings open. Abigail stands there, cheeks flushed, and eyelashes heavy with apology. "I'm so sorry," she breathes. "I got home late and - would you believe - little Marcus Iams dumped his paints on me. I looked like a walking Jackson Pollock!"

She's talking a mile a minute, but all I can see is that emerald dress clinging to her curves, how the soft fabric drapes over her hips, the way her sun-warmed thighs peek beneath the hem. My heart slams. I need to shut off her chatter and just take her in.

"Abigail," I say, low and steady, "Abigail," I repeat, raising my voice a little more. Before she can add another word, my arms wrap around her waist, fingers brushing right above the swell of her ass, pulling her flush against me. Her monologue dies with a little gasp. I tip her chin up, my palm sliding up the column of her neck, and press my lips to hers. The silk between us is so thin, I feel the swelling of her nipples peddling through, and I physically restrain myself from glazing my thumb over them, allowing myself the time I want to spend exploring her body.

Leaning back, I can tell Abigail is still in shock; hell, so am I. For a man who wants to keep us out of the public's eye, I sure did make a spectacle of us on her doorstep. I don't want to hide her, in fact, nothing would make me happier than showing up to outings around town with her on my arm, but until we know what we are doing, I want to keep us lying low for Charlie's sake. Dating before kids is significantly different.

"So that's how I get you to stop talking, huh?" My voice is lower than usual, and her wide eyes stare back at me. Before she can respond, a bellowing laugh escapes her, causing me to be confused.

Her hand flies over her mouth as she attempts to stop laughing. "I'm sorry! I have read about men doing that to a woman, but I didn't think guys really do kiss you to get you to shut up." Her hands glide up my stomach and onto my chest, bringing her even closer to me. Her kiss is so light, I wouldn't have known it happened if I blinked.

"We'd better get going, or we may never leave." I offer, knowing there is nothing more that I want to do than never leave this woman's arms. She grabs her purse, shuts the door, and slips her arm through mine. Under the stars, I guide her back to the truck and drive us toward town.

***

By the time we finish dinner, a sweet tiramisu in a to-go box sitting between us, I park on one frequently driven red-dirt road. The tailgate is down, the truck lights casting a warm pool on the ground. Abigail relaxes as we sit side-by-side and share our dessert. I never knew that eating a dessert while sitting on my tailgate could be so erotic, but I know I'm just a few short moans away from ravishing her right here. "Bringing this with us was a genius idea," she murmurs, eyes closing as the sugar hits her tongue.

In the back of the cab, I find two plastic wine cups - my daughter's emergency stash - and pour ruby-red wine into them. "I knew we weren't leaving without it when I saw how excited you got." I chuckle to myself because while I am making fun of her, all I can think about is how beautiful she looked as the candles flickered in her face.

Her feet dangle off the back of my Chevy, humming along to "Check Yes or No" as it drifts from the stereo. I stand and hold out my hand. "Dance with me?" I ask. I'm greeted with a shy nod of her head, and before she can change her mind, I wrap my hand back around her waist and pull her to her feet. On most nights, we have Charlie following us around, who will eventually fall asleep. But tonight, tonight is different. It is just me and Abigail, dancing on his red dirt road, laughing and listening to old country music.

We sway under a sky littered with stars, the country tune cradling us in softness. Her hair brushes my cheek; the scent of grapefruit shampoo mixes with the night air. We have danced countless times in the past during nights out at Meryl's but tonight feels different. Nobody will interrupt us tonight, because she is all mine.

Feeling emboldened, I lean in closer, whispering her name, as she tilts her face up. Our lips meet in a slow, deliberate kiss. I lift her, bringing her legs around my waist without hesitation. I sit her on a wool blanket Charlie left behind, the cool fibers pressing against her calves. I lean in, trailing kisses up her thigh - stopping at the hem of her dress. I watch goosebumps rise on her skin as I make the trek up her leg. Her breath hitches; a tiny moan escapes. My hand slides under the silk, finding the lace cuff of her underwear. If I had known these were there all night, we would have skipped dinner altogether. My thumb slides under the straps of her underwear until I find the warmth that has been pooling this whole time. Her pulse hammers beneath my fingertips, warm and wet. Her eyes are tracing my movements, as if she is watching her prey and deciding when to pounce.

My hand wraps around her throat, not squeezing but owning. Her breath hitches, those sweet tits heaving against my chest. I can feel her pulse quicken under my thumb, her heart racing like a rabbit. Her legs wrap around me, pulling me in, and fuck, the heat of her pussy through my jeans has me ready to rip her apart.

Our lips clash, all tongues and teeth and desperate hunger. She tastes like sweet tea and sin, a fucking deadly combination. I bite that plump lower lip, and she whimpers, her legs tightening, begging for more. She grinds against me, and I can feel how wet she is, soaking through her lace panties, driving me fucking insane.

"You're a dirty little thing, aren't you, Abigail?" I growl, sliding my hand up her thigh, pushing her skirt away. My thumb finds her clit through the lace, and she bucks against me. "Fucking drenched, Sunshine. Is this all for me?"

"I think it was the dance. You know George Strait is my favorite," she whispers into the warm night air. I know she is trying to tease me, but I'm not in the mood for it right now. She leans back to rest on her arms, allowing me more access to her.

A wicked grin rises on my face, making a smidge of fear and intrigue rise in return.

"Is that right?" I slip a finger inside her panties, feeling her slick heat. She clenches around me, greedy for more. "You're a brat, you know that, right?" Her eyes are wide, pupils blown with lust and a hint of fear. She fucking loves this. Her legs widen subconsciously, giving me more room to take her in. I take the opportunity to slip a finger inside of her, curling it just enough to reach that perfect spot.

"Not a brat, just honest," she barely gets out as I use the opportunity to rip the sleek lace off her pussy, giving me more room to take her.

"If you were being honest, you wouldn't be about to scream my name, Abigail," I add another finger into her wet cunt, still running lazy circles with my thumb, making her arch her back in the most unnatural ways. "Eyes on me, Sunshine," I command, my voice raw and hungry.

Her eyes immediately snap to mine, pupils blown wide with lust and a hint of fear that I may stop. She's a fucking vision, all that blonde hair spread out like a halo, her cheeks flushed pink. I add another finger to her tight cunt. "Abigail," I groan, my hard dick pressing against my jeans zipper, begging to be released and allowed to explore. I reach for her throat, my hand wrapping around the front, feeling her deep swallow as I pull her closer to me. I need a better view of her eyes. I quickly note just how much bigger my grasp around her delicate throat is in comparison. If I wanted, I could take whatever I wanted from her, but hurting her is not something I plan on doing.

"Abigail, I need you to tell me to stop," I beg, my fingers tightening around her throat. Her pulse flutters under my palm. "I don't want to hurt you, Sunshine," I murmur, leaning down to brush my lips against hers. "So, you better tell me to stop if it's too much." She makes another deep swallow as I apply even more pressure to her soaking tip. Her breath is ragged, but she doesn't say a fucking word. Good girl.

"Don't you dare stop, Chase," she finally gasps out, her voice hoarse from my hold on her throat. It's the green light I've been waiting for. I force my hand to release from around her neck, but only so I can put her already pebbled nipples between my fingers as I continue the desperate circles on her clit. Twisting and pulling them until I finally hear her scream my name.

Abigail's eyes are wild and hungry; her cheeks flushed with a desperation that matches my own. I push her chest, a firm, dominating force. I'll make her wait for it. "Lay down, Sunshine. Let me see what's mine."

She complies, her body quivering with anticipation. I stand over her, my cock already throbbing against my zipper, ready to fuck. But first, I need to taste her. I drop to my knees, the gravel digging in, but I don't give a fuck. All I care about is the sweet pussy in front of me.

I yank her ass to the edge of the tailgate, her legs over my shoulders. Her glistening cunt is right there, perfect and pink. I can see every fucking detail, and it's all mine. My tongue starts slow, and it's only because I need to savor every fucking drop of her sweetness before I devour every inch of Abigail's pussy. "Fuck, you taste like heaven, Sunshine," I growl as she squirms under my grip. "You like having your pussy eaten, sweet girl? You like feeling my tongue fuck that tight little hole?"

Her response is a moan, her fingers tangling in my hair as she's trying to control my movement and keep me where she wants me. Not this time, sweet girl. I'm in control now. Her body bucks under each deliberate lick as my fingers slam into her pussy with a forceful rhythm that matches the thrusts of my tongue against her clit. She's so fucking wet; it's dripping down my beard. I can feel her heat pulsing around my fingers, and the harder she grips my hair, the more primal it feels. We both like it rough.

I slide another finger deep into her cunt and watch as her back arches off the truck bed. Her grip on my hair tightens to the point of pain; it only makes me want to pleasure her more. I pump in and out of her, and before long, she trembles under my touch. Her entire body folds around me until she bursts into high, urgent cries. Every sound she makes feels like a victory and worship all at once. Chasing the high of her screams, I give her one last suck before I bite her tip and squeeze even harder around her throat. She delivers the most beautiful song to me.

At this moment, I realize I will never be able to let her go. She is my drug, and I have zero plans to quit.

As her breaths begin to slow down, I begrudgingly pull away from her, hating every second of it. Abigail reaches for me, but before I can step closer, her legs wrap back around me and pull me towards her, not giving me the option to leave if I wanted to. I slide one hand through my now crumpled hair, trying to calm the mess she has made of me. Before I can wipe her juices from my beard, Abigail's hand flies to meet mine.

"Don't you dare wipe that off. I need to taste the mess I made of myself." Before I can comprehend what she just said, her fingers wrap in my shirt, pulling me damn near on top of her. I can feel how tight her legs have gotten, holding me tight where she wants me. Both of our sexes meet perfectly, and before I realize it, I am a fifteen-year-old boy dry humping her. Her bud must have been sensitive because it takes no time for my jeans rubbing up against her core to cause her to cum for me one last time.

I force myself to pull back. "Abigail, we have to stop. I'm about to explode in my jeans, and that's not something I want to do on our first date."

Her laugh escapes her, and I question my rationality as the sound sends a tingle throughout my body.

"The first time I take you, it won't be in my truck bed. You deserve much more than that, Abigail Kline. I need to take my time with you, and I simply can't do that when some farmer may drive down this road at any moment." The words disgust me as I say them, knowing I wouldn't care if someone did see us, but I wouldn't do that to her.

She leans up on her hands, bringing her mouth closer to mine. I may be strong, but not that strong. I push my lips to hers quickly, hoping to provide her reassurance that while I may have been cold to her for years, I don't want to be now.

"No, you are right. This isn't the place, but maybe someday." She follows this up with a wink and a sly smirk. This girl is trouble, and I love trouble.

"Someday, Abigail. Someday." I laugh, grabbing her hand and pulling her back to her feet. For what feels like the millionth time tonight, my body acts on its own as I pull her close to me one more time. Her tiny arms wrap around me as I place the smallest, sweetest kiss on the top of her head. A deep sigh ripples through me, and for once, all the voices in my head telling me to keep my walls up have slowly faded to the back of my mind, and a feeling of warmth and home has nestled in instead.

"Let's get you home, what do you say?" I mumble, dreading the idea of leaving her behind as I return to dad-duty.

"Yeah, let's head back to town." Her peaceful smile as she looks back up at me fills another hole in my heart I didn't know I was holding on to.

Chapter Twelve

ABIGAIL

t has been approximately six days, five hours, fifty-four minutes, and twenty-two seconds since I road together with Chase after our date - though who's really counting?

Certainly not me. I've seen his familiar stride across town twice since that evening, but never alone with me. In the back of my mind, I still replay the moment he trailed his fingers along the curve of my back as he guided me out of the restaurant. I feel the warmth of his palm even now.

I suppose most women wouldn't dwell on the simple moments of a date, but I can't help but replay the thrilling night, frame-by-frame. The way his body pressed near mine, the taste of his lips - but it's the slow dance I savor: the gentle sway, his rough fingertips running the length of my body, the way his cologne - woodsmoke and pine - lingered in the air as he steered by hand into his. He was the perfect gentleman, a side of him I never expected but instantly adored.

Somehow, somewhere between teasing insults and awkward hellos, we graduated from mutual annoyance to outright antagonism, from random, halfhearted dance partners to late-night drives along moonlit back roads, and finally to real dates - and, yes, the scorching heat of our encounters in the bed of his battered pickup. "Don't get ahead of yourself, Abs," I scold my racing thoughts. It was only one date after all.

A soft cough shakes me back to reality. Ms. Snider, the silver-haired librarian with a fragrance of lavender and old leather books, stands beside me at the front desk. Two dozen restless kindergarteners swarm the carpet behind us like shapes of energy too small to contain.

"Oh, sorry, Ms. Snider," I stammer. "Got a little lost in my head." My cheeks warm under her snarl.

She arches a perfectly plucked eyebrow. "You were clearly daydreaming about something, or someone, you shouldn't be." Her tone is teasing, but there's steel there. "Gossip with this old lady or read that book to these little terrors."

I swallow. "No gossip today," I lie, trying for a breezy tone. I snag the storybook from her with a quick fumbling motion - barely catching myself falling on my face. I hear her snicker as I walk away, but I don't have the nerve to turn around and see if she is still watching me.

Moments later, I'm back at my desk, scanning the publishers' new releases when the deep baritone that's haunted my thoughts for days rumbles through the quiet stacks.

"Abi!" The voice is velvet and gravel. I jump, nearly knocking my mug off the desk. Before I can turn, Charlie - my cheeky nine-year-old sidekick - throws her arms around my shoulders while her strawberry-blonde pigtails tickle my ear. "Oh my gosh, it's been forever!"

I blink. "Charlie, I literally saw you yesterday." My laugh trembles between disbelief and delight.

She shrugs. "Felt like centuries." She shifts her weight, crossing her arms, that mischievous grin bright enough to shame a summer sunrise.

I whirl around, heart in my throat - and there he is. Chase is standing just past the yellow "Quiet Please" sign, backlit by the afternoon sunlight streaming through the tall windows. The slight stubble on his jaw catches the light. His faded jeans hug those long legs that never fail to make my pulse stutter. A flicker of something both amused and intense dances in his dark eyes.

"Eyes up here, Abigail," Chase says, scaring me out of the haze. I immediately find myself anytime I am around him.

I shove a curly strand behind my ear. "Sorry, I-I thought I saw something behind you." I gasp, still trying to compose myself.

Charlie's small voice joins us in our very inappropriate, but nonverbal conversation. "Nobody is back there, Abi. Are you losing it?"

Ms. Snider's voice - sharp as a bookmark's edge - cuts in. "I think our Abigail lost her marbles years ago, sweetie." The children giggle, and I can't help but be more annoyed at her than I should be.

I close my eyes, giving myself until the count of two to calm down and refocus on what is going on. As I open my eyes, I see the last set of kids scurry out while clutching baggy arms full of picture books, and the library wraps in solemn hush again. I breathe in the scent of aged paper and polish. Then I look back at him, forcing myself to release my anxious thoughts.

"Anyway, Charlie, what've you been up to? I ask, trying to shove my blush back down.

Charlie falls into step with us. "Dad finally caved and took me to Redbird's for a chocolate milkshake." She signs theatrically. "I think he just wanted me to shut up."

Chase's lips quirk into a slow smile. "If I told you to pick out a book, would that also get you to stop talking?" I know he doesn't mean it; he loves that girl more than I think she even realizes, but this is part of their banter back and forth, testing each other along the way.

The little girl rolls her eyes, ponytail swishing. Her shoe squeaks as she shuffles away. Ms. Snider drifts by, giving me a knowing squeeze on my arm. "Ah, well, I guess I will let you two very single people talk and discuss your weekend plans in peace."

Luckily, Chase can tell how awkward I feel and how speechless I am in the wake of her pointed comment. His gaze flicks to me - dangerous and warm - and takes an almost invisible step closer. I feel that tiny movement like an earthquake in my chest. My skin prickles with anticipation, my mouth goes dry. His unknowing actions mean more than he will ever know. I try to hide my anxiety as much as I can. I have known most of these people my entire life, but sometimes I wonder whether they would still like me if they knew about the sad, anxious side of me. I'm not always this fun, goofy woman; I have my own demons, but I have worked my entire life to hide that side. Would Chase even want to be with me if he knew?

He brushes a loose curl from my temple, thumb lingering at the shell of my ear. The touch sends a shockwave through my nerves. "Come back to me, Sunshine." His voice dips to a low rumble.

My breath hitches. Sunshine. My secret nickname, just for him, that no one else knows. It's a beacon in the dark corners of my self-doubt. I can't help but wonder why he keeps calling me that? I make a mental note that I can fool him just as well as anyone else.

"Sunshine," he pleads again. Before I can reply, he curls his fingers around my wrist and leads me away from the desk.

"Wait! Where are we going?" I squeak as we pass the children's shelves.

He pauses at the silent corridor of reference books, glances both ways, then pushes me lightly against a shelf of yellowing census records. My eyes are clear as I look up towards him, and his usual scowl is turned upside down; his bright smile welcomes me instead. "Ah, there you are! There is that woman who loves to be snarky with me." Calm rushes through me to the point where my shoulders physically loosen. "What were you thinking about back there?" His smile weakens just enough for all his eyebrows to scrunch together in concern.

"Nothing. Just stuck in my own head. Sorry about that." I remove my wrist from his grip and quickly try to smooth down my blue sundress before reaching for the closest bookshelf to start rearranging the already perfectly organized shelf.

Chase's body steps closer to mine, lessening the gap between us. "Do I make you nervous?" He whispers in my ear. His hot breath sends shivers down my spine, and my cheeks instantly flush.

"Chase! Stop! We are in the library." I scoff, but we both know it is an empty statement.

"I am very aware where we are, Abigail. That is why my hands have not slid under your thin dress. But don't think I considered it." His hand slides up my arm, the material of my blue sundress whispering against his denim as he closes the space between us. His leg hooks between mine, and I inhale sharply at the firm heat pressing against me.

In an attempt to sound defiant and unamused by his antics, I tip my head up to meet his, his tall frame making it more difficult than it would be with most. Mentally, I keep telling myself to stay firm and try to dismiss him, but my rebellious side can't help but think about how hot it would be for him to pick me up like he does and push me against these shelves. The thrill that someone may see us makes my already soaking panties even wetter. I'm pretty certain this man's look could make me orgasm.

"Don't look at me like that. I know damn well you are thinking about me bending you over right here and not how annoyed you are with me." One hand reaches up and pushes a stray curl behind my ear while I do my best not to melt into a puddle at his touch."

Focus Abigail Kline. Focus! "How can I help you, Sir?" My defiant words cause him to chuckle before he grabs my wrist one more time. Dragging me away from the front desk and closer to the collection of historical documents that nobody cares about, I try to stop him, but I know there is no chance I will win.

We round the corner, and this time, he fiercely pushes me against a bookshelf. His leg returns between mine, making me spread for him. Saying I was aroused would be an understatement. Both of our breaths are heavy, mingling as we take in the moment. His eyes - now a shade darker than they were just moments ago - dance over my face and slowly down my neck before finding the small amount of cleavage popping out of my dress.

His heat-rough voice is a purr in my ear. "Charlie is staying at a friend's house tonight, and Bell has begged me to go with her to Meryl's. Will I have the pleasure of seeing you there, or will I have to come drag you out of your house kicking and screaming?" His face is so close to mine that with each word spoken, his beard brushes up against me, causing sparks every time.

My pulse slams. "I wasn't planning on it." My fingers curl around a worn spine, my nails gouging faint grooves. "But if everyone else will be there…" Implying that others may realize our jabs at each other are no longer out of annoyance, but out of arousal.

"Then you'd better be wearing something short and save all of your dances for me." He demands, leaving me no choice. But let's be honest, I'm only going there for him and what he does to my body.

My lips quirk, and I tap my temple. "Won't people get suspicious?" I tease.

He laughs, a soft growl. "Only if you let your nipples get as hard as they are right now. Everyone in that damn bar will see what I do to you. Is that what you want?"

I mockingly chuckle, "You don't do anything to me. You're just… Chase."

The words are barely out of my mouth before his leg pushes up, spreading my legs even more. His fingers graze the shell of my ear before clamping over my mouth, muffling any response I have.

His other hand slowly climbs up my leg, and when he doesn't stop at the hem of my dress, my heartbeat ricochets in my ribs as I press back against him, the worn book spines rough against my back.

His thumbs find my wetness and press. A stifled moan rumbles in my throat, the thud of my heart drowning out any sense of propriety. He draws his thumb across my soaked lace, a predator savoring the taste. "Sunshine," he murmurs against my pulse point, "you'd better get used to saying my name, because you will be screaming it soon enough." He turns to look to his side, making sure nobody has followed us back here, before his thumb pushes deeper against me, making a small moan escape my covered mouth. "Do you understand me?"

My eyes lock on his. I nod, breath shallow and chest heaving as the world fades to the curve of his jaw, the hint of stubble, and the promise in his gaze.

His hand releases my mouth and, before I can collect the broken pieces of my dignity, he claims my lips in a fierce, urgent kiss. My knees threaten to buckle, but adrenaline holds me upright as he tastes me - sweet, salty, and entirely his.

At last, he breaks away. His thumb, slick with my arousal, slides into his mouth. He straightens the skirt of my dress, smooths a wrinkle at my shoulder, and tucks a stray hair strand behind my ear with gentle precision. He leans in for one last feather-light peck, then steps back and melts into the corridor.

Before he disappears, he looks over his shoulder. "Be at Meryl's by 8:30." His wink is a private joke I'll carry home with me, sitting like embers under my skin.

I remain pressed against those dusty shelves long after his footsteps fade, my body still humming with his touch, and my heart pounding the rhythm of my single greatest dance I've ever known.

Chapter Thirteen

ABIGAIL

stand in my empty bedroom under the harsh glow of the overhead bulb, fingers grazing the rod where my washed dresses dry. "What do I even wear?" I murmur to the silence. Sundays are laundry days, and I hadn't planned on leaving the house - my favorite dress is still in the wash. At the back of the closet, I discover a pale pink sundress, faded at the waist but light and fluttery. I lift it out. "I suppose that will do, huh?" Meryl's isn't fancy, and it will be dark in there, so no one will bat an eye at a simple sundress.

The heavy wooden door to Meryl's groans as I push through. Instantly, I'm met with the tang of frying grease, the sweet hiss of beer taps, and the pulse of "Should've Been a Cowboy" by Toby Keith bouncing off the low ceiling. Couples spin on the scuffed dance floor; laughter and hoots rise between half-finished pints. Around here, simple pleasures rule: cold beer, old country music, and peace. Meryl's is my sanctuary when life unravels.

"Abs! Over here." Macy's voice slices through the din. I weave between barstools and reach our table where Macy, Bell, Lucas, and Chase. My heart stutters when my gaze lands on him: dark jeans, rolled sleeves, the traces of tattoos littered across most of his arm. His hungry look sends warmth flooding through me, a reminder of the private moments we've shared - and the façade of loathing we now maintain. His sly wink says he knows exactly what I'm thinking.

I want to blur the line between act and truth. I want him closer, not across the table. I want his teasing smile, his easy laugh, the way he helps me climb into his truck, steadying me when I wobble. Instead, I grit my teeth and aim for annoyance. I don't want to act annoyed when he asks me to dance. I don't want to pretend that I find it disgusting that he pre-bought the beer he knew I would be drinking.

I fear that he doesn't want all of that, and I already know how hurt I am going to be once this all dissolves and we go back to hating each other. How am I going to survive this? I'm not jumping to thinking I am falling for him, but I can picture us together in the mundane portions of life. That is what will destroy me.

"Abigail, do you want to stab me or dance with me? I can't tell by the look on your face." Chase's gruff voice probes.

I look over at him and can tell he is trying not to smile back at me, keeping up his grumpy exterior for the others, but I can see it in his eyes. This man is going to ruin me. "Both," I taunt while doing my best to give him an equally wicked smirk.

The shake of his head lets me know I won this match, because there is nothing he can say that won't spark speculation among those at the table.

Lucas clears his throat. "Is Hayes still coming tonight?"

Chase rolls his eyes, patience thinning. "Yeah, he's on his way."

Bell snorts. "Oh, yay - just who I want to see."

Chase frowns at her sarcasm, but I doubt she's joking. Bell is dismissive of their friendship for reasons I don't understand.

"Are we really starting this so early tonight, Bell?" Chase scolds. He is clearly annoyed, but as a woman, I don't think she is being rude; I think she doesn't want to see him for much more secretive reasons.

Macy leans in. "Abs, are you gonna dance?" Her brow lifts. Sometimes I wonder if she is like Edward Cullen in Twilight and can actually read my mind.

I toss back my hair. "Eh, not sure. I don't see anyone here that would be worth my dancing skills." I reply with a smirk on my face.

"I'm pretty sure Chase..." Macy smirks, but I have to step in before she can finish that sentence.

I cut her off with a hurried breath, "Has your doctor told you how long you can come hang out in an old bar? I'm not sure this is the cleanest place to be."

Macy's hand drifts to her belly before Luke's follows. "She said that since there isn't smoking in here, it is fine. But I think my time is quickly coming to an end when I would rather have my feet propped up and reading a good book."

"I asked Meryl to change the air filter." Lucas chimes in, shaking his head and laughing. "That man looked at me and asked if I really thought he used those. That is when I told her this might be our last night here for a while." Lucas leans towards my best friend and kisses her temple.

I can feel Macy toying with the strap of my dress, giving the physical touch she can't help but give. "Don't worry, I clocked the topic change. We can discuss it later." Damn it! I thought I got out of it.

Chase extends his hand, palm up, preventing me from getting a closer look at his tattoos. I make a note to ask him more about those later. "You ready?" He asks. "Chattahoochee" by Alan Jackson starts playing over the speakers, and the mix between the catchy tune and Chase's dark eyes, I know I don't have a choice. I don't want to have a choice, either.

I hear a small "humph" escape from Macy as I stand and try to push down my dress. The moment my hand lands in his, everything around us fades away. We have danced many times before, usually in dismay, but this time feels different. He presses me tighter than usual. His fingers trace lower on my back, grazing the curve of my hip with a possessive press whenever no one's watching.

Every sway ignites me. His heated gaze drinks me in; my own pulse thumping in my ears. He leans close, breathing warm air against my neck. "If you can't tell how hard I am for you..." His voice is a low rasp; his fingers tighten. "I don't know what else to do." His eyes wander around the bar, trying not to look at me closely so he doesn't test his strength in keeping me at bay. "I can't do this, Abigail. I can't hold you in my arms knowing how sweet you taste and how loud you scream."

"Put your big boy pants on and take me then." I taunt, squeezing his hand to tease him even more.

He chuckles darkly. "You're such a brat, you know that?" He looks around, seeing if anyone is going out of their way to watch us. "I'm going to the restroom. Finish your beer and meet me back there. Knock three times."

I nod my head but I'm wondering how I will explain this to my group of friends. Unfortunately, I am pretty sure Macy is going to notice. "Oh, and Sunshine," his hands wrap back around my waist, forcefully bringing me flush to himself, making sure I know who is in charge right now. "Bring your purse. You don't want to make that walk of shame back to the table afterward." His wink makes me breathless, and the heat I feel in my chest is taking over my senses.

I collapse into my chair next to Bell, scrubbing my palms on my dress. I chug the last of the beer before standing, reaching down to grab my purse. As I do, I remind myself that while I am willing to be Chase's good girl, I still like to razzle him. I leave my purse on the table and walk towards the back.

"Abs, you good?" I hear Macy yell. Shit.

"Oh, yeah," I quickly glance around, "stomach cramps. I will be right back." I didn't stay around to hear her response. Her mischievous smile was good enough of a message.

Knock. Knock. Knock.

No answer.

Knock. Knock. Knock.

Why isn't he answering? This man drives me crazy. Did I misunderstand his directions?

I turn to walk back to the table when the door finally opens. "Sunshine." Chase's voice purrs from the dim corner. I never liked nicknames, but I will let this man call me anything he wants. The floor tiles are grimy; the single bulb flickers. But I don't care. His hand is on my back before I can hesitate, lifting my dress into a swirl of pink cotton as he sits me on the counter. His lips crash into mine, urgent and scorching, his tongue claiming mine. Electricity explodes between us as he cups my throat - gently at first, then firm enough to thrill every nerve. "How have I ignored you this long?" he murmurs. "You're the most beautiful thing I have ever seen."

With lust-filled eyes, he leans back to take me in. "Your lips are already red and swollen. I can't wait to see how they look wrapped around my cock." The thought makes me swallow deeply. A sense of anticipation washes over me as I recall the feeling of his hardness pressed against my body earlier.

"I have one request, though." I breathlessly demand. All I get in return is a shaking of his head. He is confused and annoyed that I'm challenging him right now.

"You can only choke me with your other hand." Confusion is laced across his features. "I don't want the rose thorns poking me," I advise, while I wrap my leg around his waist. "You know, your rose tattoo. It would be painful." I point to his hand, bringing his attention to the hand in question.

His confusion evaporates as the inferno in his eyes blazes. "Abigail," he growls, his other hand clamping around my throat, squeezing like he owns me. "This is your only fucking demand. Now, shut the fuck up and spread those legs. I need to see what's hiding under this dress." I barely register the cold tile until his fingers part me. His touch is precise, relentless, as he slides two strong digits inside me, probing.

The tile bites into my back as his fingers yank my dress up, exposing my soaked pussy. He doesn't hesitate; two thick digits ram into me, rough and demanding. I can barely choke out the words, "N-nothing to f-find."

"Fuck... me..." he gasps as he drops to his knees, pushing my dress up to my waist, baring me completely. His tongue, hot and wet, licks a long stripe from my ass to my clit, his fingers still pumping into me. He's not gentle, not giving me a second to adjust. He's taking what he wants, and I'm a mess for it.

A loud groan tears through me as he pulls his fingers out, shoving them into my mouth. "Taste yourself," he commands, his voice a low rumble. "If you can't keep quiet, you'll keep sucking on these." I swirl my tongue around his fingers, tasting my own arousal, loving the dirty wrongness of it.

"More," I beg, my hips rocking against his face. He growls again, the vibration sending shocks of pleasure through me. A third finger slams into me, stretching me, filling me. His tongue lashes at my clit, relentless, pushing me closer to the edge.

"Fuck, your cunt is perfect," he growls, his fingers pumping in and out of me, curling to hit that spot that makes me see stars. "Gonna fuck you so hard with my cock, you'll feel me for days." His pulses are relentless in making me fall apart with his hand between my legs. The small circle laps continue as I come down from my high. Another deep, full swipe of his tongue cleans me from my mess as he pulls my dress back down, showing humor as he looks at the new wrinkles.

"You're such a good girl." His voice is thick with lust as he eyes my swollen, spit-slicked lips. "Now both of your lips are swollen and red." His non-tattooed hand, rough and calloused, slides down my neck, leaving a trail of goosebumps in its wake. The contrast of his earlier firm grip and his gentle touch now sends a shiver down my spine. I'm not sure which one I crave more.

His thumb traces my jaw, pressing lightly against my throat. "This pretty little throat ready to take my cock?"

I give him another deep, exaggerated swallow, making his lips curve into a dirty smirk. "Swallowing won't save you, Sunshine. My cock's been waiting too long for this."

Just as my feet hit the floor, an abrupt knock at the door makes me jump, but Chase doesn't even flinch. "Go away," he barks, his voice a low growl that makes my pussy throb. Nobody's coming in - not until he's come in me.

He rips off his shirt and tosses it to the floor. "Kneel." His voice is firm, commanding. I obey, sinking to my knees on the soft fabric of his tee. He pops open his jeans, the zipper a harsh rasp in the quiet room. His massive cock springs free, already glistening with pre-cum, a row of metal piercings gleaming along the underside of his shaft. Fuck me sideways.

"Scared of a little metal, Abigail?" he teases, gripping his cock and giving it a slow stroke. His pierced shaft is a fucking weapon, ready to destroy me. And I can't wait.

"Just admiring the view," I shoot back, licking my lips. Concern and dominance war in his eyes, but I know what I want. I want him to use me, to fuck my mouth until I'm gasping for air.

He steps closer, his heavy ball swinging like a pendulum, hypnotizing me. His massive cock is proudly on display, a network of throbbing veins wrapping around the shaft like a roadmap to sin. The bastard knows I'm hungry for him.

"They won't come out if that's what you are worried about." His massive, rose-covered hand wraps around his shaft, giving it a lazy stroke. It appears to be about to explode with one thrust. "If it's too much, tap my leg. Now, open that pretty mouth if you want me to feed you my cock."

My mouth waters, and I part my lips, eager to take him in. I've never been much of a suck-his-cock-on-my-knees kind of girl, but with Chase, it's different. I want to own his cock, make him snarl my name like the feral beast he is.

He strokes himself a few more times, his hand twisting slightly as he reaches his swollen head. Then, he guides his cock downward, tilting his hips so that the thick crown nudges at my lips and pushes into my wet mouth with a groan. "Fuck, that's it," he grunts as I circle his tip with my tongue. I flick the sensitive underside and feel his thighs tense in surprise.

Before I can take him deeper, his hand fists in my hair, gripping hard and holding me in place as if asking if I'm sure about going down this path with him. "Give me a second, Sunshine," he rasps as if it's pained him to say.

I gaze up at him, eyes watering, and my tongue flicks out at the engorged head of his cock - his answering groan is worth every ounce of effort. My blonde curls are wrapped tightly in his fist -allowing him to tug just enough to make my scalp tingle.

"Don't worry, I used the hand without the rose, so the thorns don't get tangled in your hair." He amuses, but his words turn into a guttural groan as I take him deeper, feeling every vein and ridge of his cock against my tongue.

My head bobs, saliva dripping down my chin as I work him in and out of my mouth. His grip on my hair tightens, his hips starting to move, fucking my face with a rhythm that makes my pussy clench. I can taste the pre-cum leaking from his tip, the saltiness mixing with the metallic tang of his piercings.

"Fuck, Abigail," he groans, looking down at me with eyes so dark they're almost back. "You look so fucking good with your lips around my cock."

Tears stream down my face as he hits the back of my throat, but I don't gag. I relax, taking him even deeper, so deep that my nose brushes against his abs. His scent fills my nostrils, musky and male and so fucking intoxicating.

His breath hitches, his thighs trembling under my hands. I can feel his balls draw up tight and know he's close. I pull back slightly, just enough to graze his shaft with my teeth.

"Holy shit," he hisses, his head falling back. "You're a menace."

I smile around his cock, taking him deep again, humming in the back of my throat. His hips stutter, his grip on my hair bordering on painful. I can feel every inch of him, can feel the pulse of his heartbeat against my tongue.

His cum shoots into my mouth, but before I can swallow, his booming voice fills the room. "Don't swallow," he demands as he uses his thumb to push down my jaw. "I want to see me on your tongue." I open my mouth and stick out my tongue; the salty liquid tries to either roll down my throat or over the edge of my tongue. Out of everything I thought he would do, him using the tip of his dick to spread his cum all over was never something I thought would happen. "Look at what I did to you. It's a beautiful sight to see you on your knees with my cum puddled on your tongue." He uses the same thumb to push my jaw back up and gives me a nod, urging me to finally consume him.

We're in a grimy bar bathroom, the stench of piss and cheap beer wafting around us, but I've never been so turned on in my life.

I rise to my feet, trying to straighten out my dress and pray it doesn't look too obvious at what I just did. I grab his shirt, investigating for anything too gross that would prevent him from putting it back on.

"Don't worry about it, Sunshine. It was absolutely worth it." His hand pulls me closer as he places a sweet kiss on my lips. His fluctuating modes of sweet and spicy make my head spin.

Knock. Knock.

"Not done yet!" Chase barks against my mouth, but we are only able to hear aggressive mumbles back.

"Charlie is spending next Friday at Bell's house. How do you feel about coming to my place? I can make dinner, and we can sit by the firepit," he pushes strands of my hair behind my ear.

Maybe one of the largest smiles I have ever shared fills my face. This is the life I want to live. Whether it is his fire pit or his fire pit, I want them both.

"Yep, sounds good. I will bring chocolate cake for dessert."

"Deal, but just know I am having two desserts then."

Another knock, followed by muffled voices, interrupts our cute little moment, which I will relive later. Ugh! I swear, if this is Macy, I will kill her. Opening the door, I take a hard left as I shut the door behind me. "I would use the other restroom. It isn't pretty in there." I say meekly as I walk away and listen to the groans that stay behind me.

Heading back to the table, I know I look ragged, and Chase was right about me bringing my purse, but I have committed, and I will wing it if someone says anything.

"That must have been one horrible stomachache, Abs. You good?" Macy's laughter is evident, but I continue looking forward and order another beer from the waitress as she walks by.

Refusing to look back at her, I lift my glass. "You have no idea, Mace."

"Do you know where Chase went?" Macy follows, hinting she is suspicious about my trip to the restroom.

"No idea. Who knows where he went? I'm not his keeper," I try to sound as annoyed as I would have been just a mere few weeks ago, but I doubt I was successful.

As I leave, my original thought about Meryl's being a place where you can be left alone comes flooding back. Joke's on me, I guess.

Chapter Fourteen

CHASE

shake off my daughter's and sister's prying gazes and slip into the driver's seat of my truck. Why does "no plans tonight" make them suspicious? Can't a man just sit by himself, light a fire, and drink a beer? Granted, I do have plans. Many plans, but none of them need to be shared.

I persuaded my sister to let me drop off Charlie early. Before Abigail arrives, I'll run to the grocery store and straighten up the house – dust, clean empty dishes, stray toys, the works. When it comes to Abigail, I want her to feel cared for. I want to court her properly – to show her this isn't just a hook-up. Sure, I crave the sizzle, but I want something more substantial.

Already, I know I'm moving too fast, but the woman who has been my most significant annoyance has become the woman I think about before I go to sleep each night.

Just as I put the pasta in the boiling water, I hear a car driving down my long driveway. I swirl the noodles into the water before reaching for a stemmed glass to pour in a deep red wine. I planned for her to park in the garage, aware that Macy and Lucas could easily "drive by" and see her car out there. Both have already made offhanded comments about Abigail and me, so I don't trust them not to take it upon themselves to show up at my house unexpectedly.

I open the front door, glass in hand, and come to a halt. Abigail steps onto the porch, dressed not in heels or dresses, but in charcoal-grey leggings and a loose white tank. Her blonde curls are hastily gathered into a messy bun; only a hint of mascara softens her lashes. She looks relaxed and at peace, and this is the only way I want to see her moving forward.

"Are you just going to stand there drooling, or are you going to move out of the way so I can empty my hands?" Her impossibly Southern drawl is a blend of honey and steel. She stands on her toes and brushes her lips against mine, quick and teasing.

I slip my arm around her waist, lifting her lightly until her legs wrap around me, and carry her inside. I place her on the granite island, unwilling to break the kiss even to set her wine and belongings down.

My palms trace the swell of her hips under her soft tank. She arches into me as the pasta water rises, threatening to foam over the pan.

Reluctantly, I peel my lips away, reminding myself that we are in a marathon tonight. She isn't going anywhere, and I can take my time with her. I hear her light giggle as I move to turn down the stove, and I see her in my peripheral vision taking a sip of her wine. "Hopefully, you like that wine. I didn't know what to get," I add, hoping to cut the sexual tension and bring us back to the dinner we are about to have.

She curls a strand of hair around her finger. "Perfect. I'm not picky. She drifts off the island to stand beside me, pressing her palms into my lower back. "What's cooking?"

"Just pasta – but I did make the sauce from scratch." I know I have seen her eat pasta before, but my nerves catch up with me. "You like spaghetti, don't you?"

"Relax, Chase. I'd eat pizza off your floor if that's all you had." Her smile instantly calms me and warms my chest. Placing a kiss on the tip of her nose, I request she back up so I don't accidentally burn her.

She steps back, and I can't stop my gaze from roaming over the gentle curve of her ribs, the soft hollow of her collarbone. She watches me, amused.

"Has anyone ever told you about this thing with grey sweatpants?" She teases.

I arch an eyebrow, and I stare at her. "What in the hell are you talking about, Sunshine?" I ask aware I'm about to get a long, unnecessary explanation.

She rolls her eyes. "Grey sweatpants," she says, as if I didn't understand her the first time. Her insistence makes her even more charming.

"Yes, grey sweatpants, what about them?"

In annoyance, her shoulders rise and fall with her sigh. "In romance books, the hot guys always wear grey sweatpants and a backward baseball hat." Her hands fling, encouraging me to check out the clothes I put on earlier today. The rise of my eyebrows lets her know I am still lost. "Ugh, you are annoying."

I quickly reach around her and grab my ragged baseball hat and place it backward on my head. "Are you saying I'm hot?"

"Oh, you are much more than hot. But I'm pretty sure I already know that." She spanks my ass as she walks past me to sit on the barstool.

***

Dinner is effortless – pasta twirled in parmesan, more wine, and easy laughter. As grumpy as I have always tried to be around her, I am seeing how much of a mistake I have been making. What I thought was just a flippant, always-talking-a-mile-a-minute woman is really a strong and funny woman, and I can't help but hope Charlie grows up to be someone like her.

As we move onto the back patio, I drape a soft blanket over her legs and pour her fresh wine. The night air holds a pint of pine and smoke from the fire I have created. "You love kids, don't you?" I ask, nestling close.

She nods. "Yeah, I do. They are just so pure. I wish as adults we could have that innocence."

"In my opinion, Charlie is the best kid ever to exist," I muse, waiting for her to stop talking long enough so I can kiss her. "Can I ask you a question?"

There is an odd lump in my throat with uncertainty. "Of course."

Removing the blanket we were just sharing, she places a knee on each side of my legs and straddles my lap, her hips resting lightly against mine.

She laces her hands around my neck and relaxes over me. "When did you decide you didn't hate me?" Her voice trembles.

I drop my hands to her waist. "Did you really think I hated you?" She peers up at me, wide-eyed as her eyes ping pong between mine, as I realize how my grumpiness has been interrupted all these years. "I never hated you, Sunshine. I just keep everyone at arm's length because I've been burned before." I pull her closer to me, letting our foreheads rest on each other's. "I never once hated you." I release a deep sigh as I bring her lips to mine. "Haven't you noticed how mean I am to Lucas and Hayes? I make their life a living hell, but I do it because I care about them." Another kiss. "If I hated you, I wouldn't even speak to you. I never hated you."

That's when desire tightens my gut. Her thighs press against mine, and my cock throbs with a hunger that can't be tamed. I lift her, carry her inside like a caveman, my mouth hot on her neck, sucking and biting, making her mine. She moans my name, a sound that goes straight to my balls. I tear her shirt off, her hair spilling over her shoulders, wild and free.

I throw her onto my mattress, my eyes feasting on every curve. Her skin is velvet, her nipples hard beneath her thin bra. I can see her pulse racing at her throat; her breath is coming in quick gasps. She's not playing games, not trying to use me. She wants me. All of me.

She nudges my hip with her long legs, urgent and demanding. A loud chuckle escapes me. A loud chuckle escapes me as she nudges my hip with her long legs, urging me to hurry up. "I know, I know, Sunshine. But you are just so beautiful, I couldn't help myself." I grip her leggings, peeling them off, my hands rough on her smooth skin. "I don't want to rush this, Abigail. I want to savor every inch of you."

"Why?" she whispers, trying not to jump scare me.

"Because I don't want to mess this up," pausing, wondering how much to say. My hands slide up her thighs before I spread them wide, taking her in. "I like you, Abigail, so I don't want to scare you." I hook my fingers into her panties, dragging them down, revealing her glistening pussy. I can smell her arousal, sweet and intoxicating.

A tiny smile plays on her lips. "I like you too, Chase."

Hell, I can't hold back any longer. I pull her towards me, kissing her mouth as I try to tell her how I really feel without using my words. Her back bows, arching into me as a deep moan escapes her. Just like that, I went from sweet Chase to I'm about to ravage her. Without waiting, her palms rub up my sides, lifting my shirt over my head. I suck her pebbled nipples into my mouth while I untie my sweatpants, and they fall to the ground. The sweet sounds she makes with each lap around her peaks send fire through my veins.

"Lean back for me," I order, my voice already ragged with lust. Her smile widens, her breath hitching as I get rough, pushing her thighs apart like a man starved. Her pussy is a mess of wetness, glistening and ready, making my cock throb. "Look at that pretty cunt, all dripping for me." I dive down, capturing a nipple in my mouth, teasing it to a stiff peak with my tongue, pulling back to trail kisses down her ribs, her body writhing beneath me.

Her eyes meet mine, ablaze with the same inferno raging inside me. "Did I do good, Sir?" she purrs, mocking in her tone, but my cock doesn't care. It's been waiting too long for this.

"Next time, I want to see you dripping down your thighs, Sunshine." Before she can retort, my tongue is already on the most beautiful cunt I have ever seen or tasted in my life. Her thin fingers dig deeper into my sheets as my tongue continues to run circles over her clit. She tastes better than any dream I've had of this moment, and believe me, I have had many dreams about this woman.

I pull her to the edge of the bed so firmly that she gasps at the rough movement, kneeling down so I can bury my face deeper into the wet heaven between her legs. Her fingers tangle in my hair as she grinds against my tongue, making her moans loud and deep, throaty as they come from her lips. Good girl. Taking what she wants and fucking my face without shame.

"Any limits?" I pause. I've got plans for this body, but I need her green light first because once we start, there's no going back for us.

She arches her back, those pretty pink nipples of hers begging for my mouth. I give them a twist, just enough to make her gasp, while I wait for her response. "I want you to use me, Sir," she purrs, her voice breathy and hot. "Use me like I'm your sex doll."

A growl rips from my throat, raw and primal. My fingers dig into her soft thighs, spreading her wide. "Fuck me..." I groan. Low in my throat, my fingers digging into her legs as I try to brace myself. "Is that what you want from me?" Her eyes are dark and hungry, impatient by my words. I can see her pulse quicken in her neck, feel the heat radiating off her cunt. I lean in, let my breath play over her clit. She squirms, but she doesn't back down. Good girl.

"Remember, Abigail," I murmur against her lips, "if it gets too much, you let me know." I shove two fingers deep into her cunt, curl them up, and watch as her body convulses. Her scream is music to my ears. But I've got too many plans for that tight hole of hers to stay away. "And keep calling me Sir. That's hot as fuck, Sunshine."

She moans, "Sir, please -" her hips jerking as she begs for more. "Please."

"Have you ever had a pierced cock in this pretty pussy?" I ask, lightly pressing the head of myself against her slick entrance.

"No," her eyes go wide, all innocent and curious. "Will it hurt?" she questions meekly.

Her innocence is intoxicating. She knows her limits but also wants to meet me where I am. Thinking back, she has always been like that. Reaching up, I grab those stray curls, blonde and wild, wrapping them around my fist like a rope, tugging her head back just enough to see her pupils dilate. "I'm going to be really gentle with you."

My eyes dance between hers, fear creeping in that maybe she won't be okay with it once we start. "But I want you to tell me if it's too much." A second nod encourages me to slide a condom down my shaft and line it up between her legs. I rub my cock against her slit, coating myself in her wetness. "You're beautiful, Abigail," I share as I slowly slide into her, feeling her stretch around me. Her pussy widens perfectly for me, allowing enough space within her hollow walls to give a couple of small pumps into her. "Breathe for me," I remind her as I push further.

She gasps as I hit her barrier. "Does that hurt?" I hesitate, not allowing myself to move anymore until I know she is okay.

She shakes her head, her eyes glazing. "No," she breathes out. That is all I needed to hear before I push even deeper into her. Her back arches against me while her cunt pulses around me with each stroke. I thrust deeper into her until my balls are flush against her and stay there for a beat to let her feel it all.

"I fit perfectly in you. You know that, right?" I punctuate each word with a thrust, my cock swelling as it hits her spot. She feels it, too, her breath hitching, her pussy clenching around me. I set a steady pace, but it's hard to keep it slow when all I want is to pound into her, to claim every inch of her tight cunt.

My fingers dig into her hip, holding her in place as I pick up speed. She moans, a sound so sweet and dirty, it sends a shockwave straight to my balls. I slip my other hand around her throat, applying just enough pressure to make her gasp, to send her spiraling into sensation overload. Her back arches, those perfect tits thrusting up, begging for my mouth.

"Sir..." she pleads, her voice barely a whisper. "Chase, more. Give me more." My little Sunshine is greedy, isn't she? She wants it rough, wants to feel me for days whenever she moves and remembers who owns her pleasure. Her words make my dick throb, and I answer with deeper thrusts, grinding against her clit. Before I realize it, we both reach our climax, our sweat-laced bodies are stuck together in perfect harmony. Instinctually, I wish my cum was spreading in her and not stuck in a condom. All I want is to watch myself oozing out of her, proof of what she does to me. That will come in time, though.

Afterward, I curl beside her, nuzzling my cheek into her hair. My arm drapes over her waist, pulling her close. She props herself up on one elbow, watching me in the half-light.

"Chase?" she whispers into the darkness.

"Yes, Sunshine?" I reply, unsure where she is going with this.

Her small giggle follows, quickly quieting my worries. "I have never had anyone do that to me."

I press a kiss to her temple, tasting the lingering salt of our sweat. "Did you hate it?"

She rolls over to her side, suddenly more serious than she was with her giggle. Her eyes roam to my mouth, taunting me in such a serious moment. "I can't wait to do it again..." She finally says with a soft smile.

I chuckle, nuzzling her neck. "You're going to kill me, Sunshine," I whisper in her ear, giving her a tiny bite to her neck. "And I can't wait." She laughs, and I know that nothing could be more alive than this moment with her.

Chapter Fifteen

ABIGAIL

jolt awake as the moonlight slices through the curtains, and there it is, Chase's hot breath on my collarbone. His lips trail a slow, deliberate path up my chest. Each flick of his tongue and kiss strokes the fire under my skin. He moves with an insatiable hunger that I've come to crave. I arch into him as his tongue dips into the hollow of my throat, shoving my tits into his face. He takes the bait, sucking and nipping, his stubble grinding against my skin.

There's a slick heat pooling between my thighs, my body's own way of telling me that they're ready for another round. His cock is thick and throbbing, a promise against my body. He doesn't ask for permission; he takes what he wants, and I love it. With one thrust, he slides back into me, balls deep, and I'm stretched around him, filled completely. His hand clamps around my throat, fingers pressed firmly, just enough to make my pulse throb and pussy clench.

"Look at you, he growls, "already dripping for me."

His hips snap back and forth, cock driving into me with a wet, filthy sound. The pounding sound alone causes my body to tingle with an erotic expectation. His fingers, broad and strong, knead the shaft of my throat in time with his thrusts, each rise and fall perfectly tuned to the slick channel of my body. My back arches off the bed, hips lifting off the mattress, chasing that sweet, sweet friction.

When he finds that sweet angle – his cock pressing into the spot that makes every nerve ending sing – my knees tremble and my breath hitches in a broken gasp. The world narrows to the warmth of his body against mine, the wet, soft friction, the steady pounding that feels like owning me completely. And his Jacob's ladder up the most gorgeous cock I have ever seen? Wow. It is scary at first, but once he angles you the right way, your body is officially owned by him, and his dick is the magic I didn't know I needed.

"Good girl," he grunts, "take that cock." His free hand grabs my knee, shoving it up and out, opening me wide. He leans in, biting my lip, then my jaw, and finally my ear. "How many times are you gonna come for me tonight? You like that, don't you, you filthy slut?" he rasps, his words laced with kink praise. "You like it when I fuck you like a damn animal."

I manage a nod, my eyes rolling back in my head as his hands tighten around my neck harder than ever before. He's fucking me so hard now that the sound of our flesh slapping together echoes through the room like a filthy symphony.

Before I can come down from my high, his grunts ring in my ears, his thrusts becoming stronger and more frantic. At once, his eyes close as he fills me to the hilt. Slowly pulling out, the dread of our lack of contact fills me. How has this man ruined me so quickly just by fucking me the way he does? My body feels empty once he removes himself entirely from me and leans back, looking for a towel to clean me up.

After a moment, his fingers trace lazy patterns along my spine. "Why did you want to be a librarian?" His voice has shifted – soft, genuine, curious. He brushes damp hair from my forehead; his pale blue eyes search mine with an intensity I rarely see directed at me beyond our wild encounters. Most men don't care about the more serious stuff from a woman, but this man wants to know everything about me, plus some.

I swallow, heart fluttering with the unfamiliar tug of something tender. "Oh... that's a long story," I mumble, tracing circles on his chest. "Not sure you want all the details."

"I want them all, Abigail." He cups my face, brushing his thumb over my cheekbones, anchoring me. "Tell me everything."

My throat tightens as memories I've buried rush forward. I draw a shaky breath. "My childhood... wasn't perfect. My dad was never around – always somewhere else, with someone else. It left me with a lot of darkness, trust issues... things no kid should endure." I let out a slow sigh, shutting my eyes and counting to twenty to slow my heart rate. "But I had a therapist who helped me stop the cycle. It doesn't haunt me like it used to."

"Look at me, Sunshine." Chase's large hands tilt my jaw up and turn me towards him. Facing him while I face my own past. "I'm listening, Sunshine." His voice is gentle, unwavering.

I find steadiness in his warmth. "I've survived every kind of abuse you can imagine. I refuse to let it define me. Instead, I decided to face it head-on and break the pattern." My words feel stronger when spoken aloud. He presses a soft kiss to the tip of my nose, and I relax into the confession.

"I was especially close to my uncle before he passed. He pushed me to rise above it all and be whatever I wanted. If I couldn't find the courage myself, his faith in me continues to push me."

A tear slips down my cheek before I notice it. I didn't even realize I was crying. He brushes it away with his thumb.

"You're worth every good thing," he convincingly states. "I'm sure there are others who love you without question; they just don't know how to show it.

"No," pausing, choking down my emotions so my frustration with this constant statement doesn't ruin the mood of the night. "People say they love me unconditionally, but they love to hold 'conditions' over my head. When someone messes up, that shouldn't mean you bring it up all the time or remind you of your faults."

We hold each other in the quiet. Then I managed to answer his original curiosity. "I became a librarian because books saved me. They were my escape hatch from the chaos. Helping someone else find that escape – that's why I do it now." My fingers run through his mussed hair and try to tame the strands that are standing up. "What if I could help someone else escape into a book when they are going through those things we don't say out loud? That's what fuels me now."

He smiles, pride softening his rugged features. "That's admirable. You want to give people hope."

I shrug, "I'm not a hero – just doing my part in this little town."

He nods and carefully asks, "And your parents now?"

"My dad?" I shake my head. "No relationship. Removing him was proving to myself I'm worth more than his neglect."

A meek smile widens his face. "Yeah, I get it. Those types of decisions aren't ones that people like to respect either."

"I have never seen your mom around town. Does she live around here or is she far away?" I counter, hoping to pivot away from the topic of me.

He laughs, a brittle edge beneath the sound. "I don't know where she is, and frankly, I don't care. She's done me no favors."

I always assumed Chase had a story behind his ice blue eyes and grumpy demeanor, but when I asked around, nobody really knew what it was. "What happened?" I ask.

Releasing a sigh, Chase hesitantly continues. "When I graduated from high school, I decided to go to college in Austin. I spent more time partying than studying, and before I knew it, I found myself skipping class to experiment with drugs. That's how I met Charlie's mom, Anna. She was involved with the party scene, and before I realized it, she was telling me she was pregnant. I dropped out the next day and started working on the oil rigs. I wanted to provide for my child in a way that my own parents didn't."

I hug him tighter, placing tiny kisses on his shoulder. "I'm sorry. I can't imagine having to change my entire life trajectory like that." My heart aches at the memory in his eyes.

He shrugs, half smiling. "It's okay. I wouldn't do it any differently. Charlie is my entire world."

"Was your mom around to help when she was a baby?" I probe, wondering how he got here without any family around him other than his sister.

He would never admit it, but the sadness in his eyes will be something I won't forget about. "The opposite, honestly." His mind wanders as he searches for his words. "When I told her that Anna was pregnant, I asked if I could move back in with her and Bell until I saved up enough to rent our own place. She laughed in my face." He shakes his head as if he is reliving the shocking revelation all over again. "She told me she didn't want me, Bell, or "that baby" anywhere around her and didn't care where we ended up. When I left that night, I took Bell with me, and we moved off."

I feel an overwhelming sense of sadness for them. I can't even imagine being Bell and having my brother pack up my things and leave my mom behind.

"There was no other option. I wasn't going to leave Bell there to deal with our mom alone. So, I took her as a teen and then quickly had a newborn child."

"Where is Anna now?" I ask. Not sure if I want the answer.

Chase shakes his head in humor, but his eyes show sadness. "I don't know. I get a text from her about every nine months. I don't respond unless it is directly about Charlie. She never responds. I gave up on her a long time ago. She never put the drugs down, and I refuse to allow Charlie around that."

"If she got clean, would you let her back in Charlie's life?"

His shrug is hesitant. "Only if she could prove she was clean, had a job, and could show me that she could be consistent. But I don't see that happening any time soon."

"I'm sorry. Not only did you have to drop out of school, get kicked out of my mom's house, but you had to become a single dad while also trying to juggle being a brother-turned-dad to a teenager." I squeeze his shoulder, letting him know I am here for him. "I can't imagine."

"No need to be sorry. I did what I had to do." His last words hang between us as we both process this new knowledge together.

Desperate to change the sad mood, I joke, "On a lighter note, I think I found my least favorite quality about you." I tease, grinning as I push him over to allow myself to straddle him and pin his hands above his head.

His laugh sends a shiver down my body. "Oh, yeah? Enlighten me."

I can't help myself as my smile widens over me. I love that he is letting me pretend I am in charge right now. We all know this hunky man could flip me over before I counted to one. "You went to Austin. Honestly, that was your biggest downfall. Everyone knows you go to Norman if you want to get a good education…"

Without notice, Chase proceeds to flip me over, now straddling me and pinning my arms together, mimicking what I did to him just seconds earlier.

"You're full of shit, Abigail Kline." We both burst into laughter, and the sweet sound warms my heart.

"It's okay, though. We can't all be perfect." His mouth slams into me before I can fully complete my sentence.

Right when his tongue slides into my mouth, we both jump as the front door slams shut with a thunderous crack. We snap apart, staring at each other, unsure of what just happened.

"CHASE!" We freeze and stare back at each other. Bell's voice rings through the room, urgent and unmistakable.

Our whole relationship is about to be found out.

Chapter Sixteen

CHASE

What the actual fuck is my sister doing here? My pulse spikes as I realize she should be with Charlie. Is everything okay? I shake off the thought and scramble out of Abigail's arms, my bare feet skidding on the cool hardwood. I pat across the room for my stray sweatpants – our earlier frenzy left my clothes scattered like confetti – and finally find them crumped under the armchair. I mutter, "Sorry," as I yank them on before turning to walk down the hallway, shutting the bedroom door with a click.

"Bell, what's wrong?" I call into the hallway, my voice tight, every second stretching.

Standing frozen in front of me, her brow furrowed. We stare, stunned – our mirrored expressions a testament to how unthinkable this all is. "I thought you were having a manly night alone," she offers hesitantly, her eyes flicking up and down

over the scratches and faint welts across my chest –
Abigail's souvenir.

"We'll get to that later. Where's Charlie?" My
heartbeat ratchets louder.

"We are 100% coming back to this," she declares
while her eyebrows raise. "She's in the car. She's
been throwing up, and I can't calm her down."

My stomach twists. "Shit! Okay, I'm going to go
get her." I brush past Bell and head out into the crisp
air. The moonlight glints off the dewy grass as I
hurry to the driveway.

When I return, Bell and Abigail are face-to-face
in the living room. Abigail's cheeks burn scarlet, and
she's clutching my duvet cover to hide what little
she's still wearing.

"Am I reading this right?" Bell turns to me;
disbelief etched into every line of her face.

Abigail is silent, her wide eyes begging me to
speak. I clear my throat. "Yes, you are, Bell. Now
move, please – Charlie needs the couch." Irritated, I
gesture toward the sofa. Bell steps aside, but leans in,
curiosity blazing. My irritation doesn't come from
Charlie being sick, but more from how
uncomfortable Bell is making Abigail feel.

"Are you two dating? Is she your girlfriend... or
just friends?" Bell's questions are rapid-fire amid the

chaos. "How long has this been going on? When were you going to tell me?"

I cut her off before the questions kept avalanching. "I don't know. I hope she wants to be. It's been a little while. I planned to tell you after – well, after we decided everyone should know."

My words hush Bell, and a breathless silence follows. Then Abigail's shy voice breaks through like sunlight. "If I want to be?" She half smiles, despite the blush on her cheeks.

"Yeah," I say, "if you want to be." My heart hammers as she nods, and at that exact moment, I hear a muffled cry from.

"Dad!"

Instantly, I switch to parent mode. I whisk past Abigail, scoop up my little girl, clutching her stomach, and set a small plastic bin beside her. She moans softly but manages a weak smile when she spots Abigail watching over us.

Bell clears her throat. "Okay, well, I'm going to head out. I think I caused enough of a disruption here tonight." She brushes past and presses a quick hug into Abigail, who giggles despite the awkwardness. As the door clicks shut, the tension in the room evaporates in Abigail's laughter. I'm thankful she can see the humor in this because this is not how I pictured telling our friends and family.

"I'll get water and crackers," she says, trying to keep her laughter to a minimum.

I settle Charlie onto the couch with a damp washcloth on her forehead. "Dad," she whispers, voice still soft, "are you really... dating Abi?"

I cup her cheek and search her eyes. "I want to, but is that okay with you?"

"Duh, Dad. It's about time." She barely gets the words out before she grabs the trash can.

Abigail stays close, leaning into the arm of the sofa until Charlie's breathing evens out and she drifts to sleep. "Do you want me to go?" she whispers into the still room.

I gently tug her back down beside me and press a soft kiss to her hair. "I don't want you to – but I understand if you want to." The words I don't say are that I never want her to leave.

She curls against me, warmth radiating through the fabric of my shirt. "No. I think I'll stay." Her voice is a hush as she lifts her head. "Do we tell everyone now?"

I stroke her cheek and glance around. My daughter is fully asleep, my hair mussed from the night's chaos, Abigail wearing one of my old band shirts she stole from my dresser. "I doubt Bell made it past my property lines before sending out a mass text, but yeah. Yeah, I think we should go ahead and tell them."

Abigail nods, but moments later, she is drifting off to sleep, only signaled by the deep breathing and small snore. I lay back, content in the soft glow of the lamplight, both girls curled against me like puzzle pieces.

Morning light slants through the curtains, and my phone buzzes with a flood of messages - from Bell demanding details and friends with excited or shocked emojis. I shuffle into the kitchen, brew strong coffee, and snap a picture of Charlie and Abigail cozied up on the couch, clutching mugs. Their laughter at some cartoon quip is the soundtrack to my contentment.

Later, I texted back that we'll join the group at Meryl's the following weekend. Charlie, now pink-cheeked and bright-eyed, chimes in to make sure I'm still serious about dating Abigail. I rack my brain through her priority list, wanting her to understand that if this is something she doesn't want now – or in the future – all she has to do is tell me. I am relieved when she was consistent in her answers and gives me the thumbs up.

"Do you think my friends at school will think I'm cooler now that they know the 'hot librarian' is dating my dad?" She asks, a tone of comedy laced between her sincere questions.

My eyebrows raise as I gauge how serious she is. "Wait, kids call me the 'hot librarian?'" Abigail amuses, giving me a wink as if I will consider a group of nine-year-olds as someone who will take my woman.

Charlie dramatically nods her head. "Yeah, that's why all of the boys like to go to the library all of the time."

"Well," Abigail laughs while ruffling my daughter's hair, "at least I'm doing something right to foster a love of reading."

I shoot her an exasperated look, and she rolls her eyes, high-fives Charlie, and I feel like my heart may burst.

We end up convincing Abigail to stay through dinner and a movie. Charlie begs for a sleepover, but we decide we're not rushing – my daughter's sense of security matters most.

Finally, I walk Abigail to her car, the porch light haloing her silhouette. I press her against the cool metal, inhale the scent of her shampoo, and plant gentle kisses along her neck. Goosebumps rise on her skin, a soft moan slipping past her lips. My pulse surges; I know we shouldn't – but I crave every second. "Don't Chase. I won't be able to stop you." I nibble her ear as a response, and the teasing gesture doesn't go unnoticed.

"But my Sunshine, I need you to give me something to daydream about while I take an extra-long shower later," I whisper, sliding my hand beneath the oversized tee she stole. I brush aside her bra and toy with her nipple until it pebbles beneath my fingertips, then pull away with a laugh at her mock annoyance. "Oh, I told the group text we would be at Meryl's next weekend. You good with that?" I call back at her as I watch her give me a pout.

She rolls her eyes, and I pretend I don't see it. "Do I get a drive around the back roads afterward?"

This woman asks the stupidest questions. "Only if you wear a dress and no underwear..." Her cheeks flame red instantly as I chuckle to myself, and I continue back to tend to my daughter.

Since I didn't get any arguments, I take it that it's a yes.

Chapter Seventeen

ABIGAIL

'm standing in front of my closet beneath the soft glow of the bedroom lamp, fingers hovering over satin and lace, silk and cotton. Each dress sways on its hanger like a promise, but none feels quite right. Chase's mischievous instruction of "no underwear" echoes in my mind, and a wicked thrill pools in my belly. Tonight, I want to tempt him, make him ache for every inch of me until he can't see straight.

I scoop up my keys from the entryway table and tap Macy's contact. "Emergency," I say when she answers. "My closet is failing me, and Chase is expecting me tonight."

Her laughter bubbles through the speaker. "Look at you, all worked up over outfits now. Chase Travers has you wrapped around his finger, doesn't he?"

Heat flushes my cheeks. She's not wrong, which only makes it worse.

"Are you helping me shop or not?" I press my lips together, refusing to give her the satisfaction of knowing she's struck a nerve.

Her laughter winds down into a sigh. "Fine, fine. I'll help you seduce the man. Get over here in ten minutes."

The streetlamps cast long fingers through evening mist as I navigate the familiar route. When Macy and Luke's house comes into view - that craftsman with the wrought-iron planters and the wind chimes she insisted on hanging despite Luke's protests—something tightens in my chest. My foot eases off the gas pedal. This is what waits at the end of the fairytale: not just a house, but a home with the right person, a nursery being painted, a future taking shape.

Macy steps onto the porch, her belly preceding her like a proud announcement beneath the glow of the porch light. She'd sworn off Meryl's until after delivery day, but here she is, lured by the promise of vicarious excitement through my evening with Chase.

The car hums along as we head back toward town, Macy studying my profile in the dashboard glow. "So, what exactly are we shopping for tonight?"

I run my tongue across my lower lip, choosing my words. "Something that leaves little to the imagination, but still decent enough for the public. I'm skipping the undergarments entirely."

George Strait croons through the speakers, filling the sudden quiet. Macy's eyes widen. "Wait— you're going completely bare under your dress? Nothing at all?"

I shrug, heat creeping up my neck. "Yes, Macy, I am. This man drips sex, and I want to make sure I do as well." I retort, knowing I am shocking her because I never talk like this.

Her laughter bounces around the walls of my vehicle. "So small that you can meet him in Meryl's back bathroom like you did a couple of weeks ago and then come back out and pretend that everything was normal before you left?" Her nonchalance irks me. I hate that she put this together on her own.

I find the perfect outfit and rush home to get ready, making sure I don't skimp on shaving or lack of underwear. I step through the threshold of the old bar as the neon sign buzzes overhead and a swirl of hazy smoke snakes from the open door. Inside, folks cling to the bar, and the beat of country music pulses through the air. I scan the crowd – no sign of Chase yet. I settle at the bar before ordering myself a drink.

A solid arm slides around my waist. Before I can turn, his hot breath teases my neck, and goosebumps rise along my collarbone.

"Will I find underwear underneath that dress, Sunshine?" His growl sends heat through me, making me fight the urge to grab his arm and walk out of the bar now and not later.

I turn and offer a sly smile, meeting his dark eyes. "No, Sir, you won't." I let my fingers trace the edge of his shirt. "Does that make me a good enough girl to reward me later?" I swear I feel him reach his hand up to wrap around my waist before dropping it again. I choose not to let that bother me since I know this whole dating thing is new for us. "Or will my not wearing a bra provide you with more motivation?"

He shifts closer, the warmth of his body pressing against mine. "And here I thought you were a good girl." He murmurs, voice husky. "But really, you are my good girl." This time, he allows his hand to rest low on my waist. If I didn't know better, I would swear he is slowly trying to pull my dress up higher and higher, looking for a peek.

Chase rolls his lips into a slow grin. Then, with a decisive flick of his wrist, he spins me around and pins me to the bar's polished wood surface, littered in scrapes and drink spots accumulated over the years. Cool light from the overhead bulbs illuminates every curve of my body – every hold he keeps as his eyes roam from my collarbone to the hem of my dress. My pulse flutters in my throat: I want nothing more than to vanish with him in front of everyone here.

"Quit thinking so loud, Abigail," he whispers. His familiar laugh, rough-edged and warm, rippled around me. Nearby patrons glance over, curiosity sparking in their eyes when they realize whose laugh it is for the first time. Their shocked faces remind me that most don't know what it sounds like because of his stern demeanor. I forgot about that side of him so quickly in the last couple of months. One of those simple normalcies that he keeps just for me.

"Mr. Travers," I advise while meeting him toe-to-toe, my breasts meeting his chest and forcing him closer to me. "I think you should finish your drink and give me a dance before we get too distracted." I slide my finger through his belt loop to make sure he doesn't escape.

I can't hear his annoyed growl, but I definitely felt the vibration from his chest. I take a slow gulp of my drink, but before I can even swallow, Chase has emptied his beer and is yanking me by my hand, leading me to the dance floor. His hands wrap around my waist while "Fishin' in the Dark" by the Nitty Gritty Dirt Band drifts through the speakers. His body is solid, protective, and every sway forces me to let go of tension I didn't know I carried.

It feels like we're alone beneath the spotlight, the murmur of the bar receding as he presses a soft kiss to my lips. I have ached for this feeling for my entire life. I have fallen so far for this man; I hope it doesn't all fall apart right as I get used to it. "What are you thinking about, Sunshine?" He whispers in my ear.

I meet his gaze, chest rising and falling against his shirt. "How happy I am right now." The confession tumbles out before I can stop it, but the way his smile breaks across his face—slow and genuine—makes the vulnerability worth it.

I press my lips to his ear, my breath catching as his stubble grazes my cheek. "Do you think we've made it obvious enough that we're together, or do they need one more song?" I chide, my fingers trailing along the damp collar of his shirt where sweat has begun to bead. The heavy scent of his cologne mingles with whiskey on his breath. Not so secretly, I want him to drag me out of here over his shoulders, his calloused hands gripping the backs of my bare thighs, but I'm sure he'll want to torture me just a little bit more - make me wait until my skin feels like it might catch fire under this thin dress.

His mouth captures mine again, deeper this time, his kiss lingering until my knees nearly buckle. A flush of heat pulses through me, pooling low in my belly, making me acutely aware of how exposed I am beneath this thin dress. "One more dance," he murmurs against my lips, "then we're leaving." Right on cue, the tempo shifts to a slow, sultry tempo. His arms tighten around me, pulling me flush against him as we sway. When the final notes fade and the next track begins, we break apart and make our way toward our friends waiting at the table against the far wall.

The music changes to something faster as we weave through the crowd back to our table. Lucas raises his beer in greeting while Macy's fingers flutter a welcome. From the far side, Hayes stretches his neck like a curious rooster, his mouth falling open when he spots us. "Since when are you two a thing?" he hollers over the din, eyes darting between us. "Chase, you sneaky bastard!"

Heat crawls up my neck to my cheeks as Hayes' words hang in the air. Chase just settles deeper into his chair, his arm finding its way across the back of mine while his fingertips draw invisible patterns against my skin. "Careful there, Hayes," he says with that sideways grin of his. "Don't go putting ideas in her head about trading up." The low rumble of his laugh follows, and something inside me melts at the sound—a rare treasure he doesn't share with many.

The group quickly settles into the normal pace of our group, teasing and annoying each other at the same frequency. The history of our group flickers in my eyes, reminding me how much we have all grown in the last couple of years. The difference is startling if you start comparing.

Bell and Hayes are the only single ones left at the table, Chase's best friend since childhood, sitting directly across from her. They don't look at each other, not even accidentally. Their careful orbiting makes me wonder if they once collided—maybe in high school when everyone was figuring things out. Now there's this deliberate space between them, like two magnets pushed to opposite sides of the table. They're working so hard not to notice each other that it's impossible not to notice.

Hayes catches my eye from across the table. "Abs, how about another spin around the floor?" The invitation hangs there, deliberate as a matador's cape. Lucas shoots him a look that could freeze whiskey, a silent "don't poke the bear" warning that Hayes pretends not to notice. But that's Hayes - a man who makes his living getting thrown from two thousand pounds of fury isn't about to tiptoe around Chase's newfound territorial streak where I'm concerned.

Chase rises to his feet, drawing me up alongside him. His chest puffs out like a rooster's as I slip my arm around his waist. "I think my girl's had enough dancing tonight," he announces, his drawl carrying across the bar with unmistakable possession. The corner of my mouth twitches with both annoyance and pleasure as I tug him toward the exit, our fingers interlaced and his thumb stroking my palm in silent promise.

Chapter Eighteen

CHASE

The door to Meryl's barely shuts behind us, and before Abigail even has a chance to catch her breath, I sweep her around the corner and press her back against the rough brick wall. Her perfume – honeyed vanilla with a hint of sun-warmed grass – floods my senses. I let my gaze drift over the soft curve of her cheek, down the gentle swell of her collarbone, and across the smooth canvas of her limbs. The chill of the night air against my exposed arms only sharpens the heat between us; I feel goosebumps prickle her skin beneath my stare.

My fingers trace the line of her thigh, sliding beneath the hem of her dress. When I reach the apex of her thigh, I find bare, smooth skin, confirming she obeyed my secret instruction. "Good girl, Sunshine," I purr, my breath tickling the nape of her neck. Her nipples tighten against my palm, pressing through the thin fabric of her dress. She swallows hard, eyelids heavy as she meets my gaze.

"You like being my good girl, don't you?" I murmur, my voice rumbles low.

Her slender hand encircles my wrist and gently – but firmly – pulls me away. The dress falls back into place, and I feel my pulse spiking, my hardness pressing insistently against my jeans. I flip her dress back up, teasing her bare pussy with my fingers. Her breathing hitches. "Yes, Sir," she whispers, her voice soft as moth wings. "But you know I like to be an overachiever."

"Is that so?" I smile wickedly, ready to take on that challenge. "Let's go for a drive." I scoop her up, tossing her over my shoulder. We stride down Main Street under the glow of the streetlamp, her dress fluttering up in a breeze, showing off her perfect ass. I spank her lightly, and she lets out a moan that anyone on Main Street could hear if they listened just right. I reach up and cover her bare pussy with my free hand, savoring the warmth there.

Once inside my truck, I rumble out onto the dirt road with our windows down. I wind tangles through her golden hair, and she sings along with the radio – soft, half-remembered lyrics that break my tension. Fields of wild sunflowers line both sides of the road, their yellow heads nodding in time with our passing.

I reach across the console and take her hand. Nothing simpler or more perfect exists at this moment.

But mid-drive, I feel her shift beside me. She unbuckles her seatbelt and flips up the center console divider with a coy glance. "What are you doing, Sunshine?"

Her eyes flash to mine, a wildfire burning through her long lashes, incinerating any last shreds of self-control. She's a vision, and she knows it. "Just keep driving. I have an idea." Tugging off my belt, weaved through my belt loops, and opening my jeans, the zipper growls as she drags it down, slow and deliberate. "Eyes on the road, Sir," she coos, her voice honey and velvet. Her hand wraps around my thick shaft, and I grit my teeth against the longing that surges through my body.

"Fuck... me..." I grunt as I look at the road and lean my head back. I try to reposition to make it easier for her, but she just swats my thigh with her free hand. She lets me be in charge in the bedroom, but I guess she will be the one in charge when I'm driving.

She dips her head, and I hiss as her hot, wet tongue licks a stripe up my cock, tracing the metal rods of my Jacob's ladder. She swirls her tongue around the sensitive spot just under my head, making me jerk like I've been hit with a live wire. This girl is learning what makes me tick, and it's sexy as hell.

She takes me deep, her head bobbing up and down, the lights from the dashboard playing off her pretty face. She hums around me, the vibrations shooting straight to my balls. I can see the glint in her eyes, the wicked smile playing at the corners of her mouth stretched wide around my cock.

"That's it, my Abigail," I grunt, trying to keep my eyes on the road while she blows my mind. "Take that cock like a good girl."

She moans, the sound sending shocks of pleasure straight to my core. She starts to gag as I hit the back of her throat, but she doesn't pull back. No, my girl pushes forward, taking me deeper until her nose brushes my leg.

Abigail's head is in my lap, her mouth stuffed full of my thick cock. She's not just sucking me off; she's fucking worshipping it. The sight has me gripping the steering wheel like a vise.

The dash lights cast a dirty glow over her face, shadows dancing as she deepthroats me. She pulls back, gasping for air, a string of spit clinging to her lips before she dives back down, chasing her prize. "Fuck, Abigail," I grunt, the truck rumbling down the gravel road. "You're a goddamn vacuum, aren't you?"

She giggles around my cock, the sound vibrating through my balls. I can feel the cum churning, ready to explode down her throat. She senses it too, her eyes flicking up to meet mine, daring me. "Don't even think about stopping," she growls, pulling off just long enough to speak before she's back at it, her head bobbing faster, sloppier.

I slam my foot on the gas, continuing our descent down the dark road. Who am I not to follow directions? I speed back up, gripping the wheel until my knuckles are white, willing myself to focus on the rough gravel beneath the tires.

The world narrows to her mouth, her rhythm. I count the sunflowers until my vision blurs. Then warmth blooms low in my belly at the sound of her choking on my cock. A hot gush fills her mouth; I can't help the groan that rips free. Remembering what I demanded from her in the past, she lifts her head up and slowly opens her mouth. I see my cum pooling there, ready to be devoured by my Sunshine. Once she receives my sign of approval, she swallows carefully, tilting up a triumphant smile. My hands shake, but I pull the truck over anyway, unable to resist her any longer.

I reach over, drawing her to me for a kiss. Out here on these back roads, we're alone with just the stars and silence. Not another soul for miles - no headlights to interrupt what comes next.

Her giggle fills the cab of the truck as she pulls away. "Want to dance?" She asks, thinking that is what I care about right now.

"The only dance I wanna see is you riding my cock, Sunshine." Her eyes widen, pupils dilating. I fist her hair and growl into the shell of her ear. "Now sit on my lap like a good girl and call me Sir when I make you scream."

I slide the seat back, flip the wheel up, and she crawls over, straddling me. Her bare pussy presses hot against my thigh. Leaning forward, I nudge her dripping folds. "Did choking on my cock get you this dripping wet, Sunshine?"

The truck cab is filled with the wet sounds of her pussy as I thrust two fingers deep. She arches, eyes fluttering closed. I fuck her with them, curling to hit that spot that makes her scream. She clamps around me.

"Fuck, you're tight," I grit out, edging the need to slam into her right here. Easing my throbbing cock toward her entrance, I glide myself through her juices, trying to remember the feeling of feeling her bare for future use. I mindlessly dig in my truck door for a condom, and while I am ripping it open between my teeth, my girlfriend slides just the tip in her. It takes everything in me not to thrust up. The thought of feeling all of her, skin-to-skin, nothing keeping me from her, sends a tearing groan from deep in my chest. I want her like that, but I don't think we are there yet. Well, I'm sure she isn't, but I know for a fact I am. She rocks her hips before I lift her up and slide a condom on before I lose all control.

"Nice and slow, baby," I command, grabbing her hips and easing her down on my cock, inch by thick fucking inch. Her walls grip me like a vise, and it's all I can do not to slam up into her. But no, I want to savor this. Make it last till our bodies are slicked with sweat and cum every last drop of pleasure out of each other. Her nails dig into my shoulders, breath hitching as she takes all of me in and begins to roll those hips like a goddamn dream grinding into me; back arches; tits push into my face.

I let her settle for a moment, then begin a slow, deliberate rhythm. Her back arches; she moans into my mouth when I suck a kiss onto her collarbone. I bury my hands in her hair and pull her closer, thrusting until her body bounces upon mine. She's so wet, so ready – my every movement meets hers in perfect harmony. I whisper, "You're perfect, Sunshine," each syllable muffled by passion.

I tug her dress down with calloused fingers, freeing her breasts as she moves above me. Earlier, she'd teased about going braless, but I hadn't believed she'd actually show up at Meryl's wearing nothing underneath. The realization that she's been this bare all evening, this wild, makes my heart stutter with something more profound than just desire.

Her head rolls back, arching her spine like a cat in heat, offering those sweet tits to my hungry mouth. I latch onto her hard nipple, sucking it in like a man possessed, my tongue lashing it like a whip. "Fuck yeah, ride that cock, Abigail. Show me what a good little slut you are." Her name rolls off my tongue like a dirty prayer, as she bounces on my dick, faster and harder.

I can feel her pussy gripping me tight, her walls squeezing my shaft like a velvet vise. She's close, so fucking close. I growl, biting down on her nipple, just enough to send her over the edge. Her body convulses, bucking and shaking like a wild mustang, as she screams her release to the Texas sky.

"That's it, baby," I grunt, gripping her ass cheeks harder, spreading them wide as I fuck up into her like a piston. "Come all over my big cock."

Her pussy clamps down on me, milking me for all I'm worth. I can feel her juices gushing out, coating my balls, dripping down my shaft. It's so fucking hot, I can't hold back any longer. My cock explodes, pulsing rope after rope of thick, warm cum. One day, I will get to spill into her, have her feel me deep inside her, and pray that my seed finds where it belongs. I want to mark my Abigail in that way, a permanent reminder that she is mine.

I grab her throat with one hand, pulling her down so we're eye to eye. Our breaths mingle, hers ragged and desperate. "You take every last drop like a good girl," I rasp, feeling her throat bob as she swallows hard against my palm. My other hand is still gripping her ass, fingers digging into her flesh as I grind her against me, making sure she feels every inch of my cock throbbing inside her.

Her eyes roll back as she licks her lips, moaning softly and sweetly. "Yes, Sir," she whispers, her body shuddering one last time before melting into me.

Our bodies slowly calm down together, still sticky with sweat. Before she gets off my cock, I grab a handful of napkins and hand them to her. I am thankful I keep a few of them in my truck for emergencies. She laughs through her blush and cleans us both off. Moonlight pools across the truck as I ask, "Ready for that dance?"

Her face turns to look at me. Her smile is wide as she asks whether she can choose the song. I think it's funny she thinks I will tell her no. I jump out of the truck and go around the front to open her door for her. She uses my hand to step out as I lace my fingers between hers. The radio spins a slow ballad, and we sway under a constellation of fireflies and stars, the warm breeze easing every ache in my body.

Chapter Nineteen

CHASE

The **radio turns** to white noise as I pull down the tailgate and reach for the emergency blankets I keep stashed behind my seat. Before long, we're lying flat beneath a canvas of stars, her bare leg draped over mine, naming constellations we probably get wrong. She's telling me about something wild she did with Macy when my attention drifts to the scattered freckles dotting her cheeks and nose. My index finger hovers just above her skin, tracing imaginary lines between them. It's only when her story trails off that I notice her lips moving silently - ten, nine, eight - a rhythmic countdown repeating itself as her eyelids flutter closed, like she's trying to picture something just beyond my understanding.

I brush my fingertips along her forearm, feeling goosebumps rise beneath my touch. "Talk to me," I whisper. "Where'd you go just now?"

She exhales, her eyes finding mine. "It's this thing I do. The counting. Helps quiet everything when it gets too loud up here." She taps her temple with two fingers.

I prop myself up, studying her face in the starlight. "Whatever storm's brewing in there, I want to be there with you."

She rolls onto her side, one hand tucked beneath her cheek. "Most days, I'm good at keeping the monsters caged. But sometimes..." Her voice softens. "Sometimes the mask slips. I've gotten pretty good at gluing it back on before anyone notices."

Her words hang between us in the cool night air, both weightless and heavy at once. I draw her closer against me, her body fitting perfectly into the curve of mine. "With me, you don't need masks," I whisper against her hair. "I want all of you—even the parts you think you need to hide."

"When did it start?" I ask softly. "The anxiety."

Her shoulders lift slightly under my arm. "Forever ago, maybe. It comes and goes, but changes trigger it - even good ones." There's a pause where my heart stops, thinking she might say I'm the trigger, but then her fingers find my forearm and squeeze gently. "Like this. Us."

Crickets harmonize with the static-laced music still drifting from my truck radio. Moonlight bathes her face, illuminating the constellations of freckles across her skin. I trace one with my thumb. "Is it weird that I call you Sunshine?"

She shakes her head; a laugh caught in her throat. "No. But I'm curious - why that nickname?"

My mouth goes dry. The question feels loaded now, dangerous. "It's just whenever I see you, you're this bright spot. Like everything else fades a little."

"We all have our demons, Chase." The playfulness has vanished from her voice.

"Maybe, but somehow you always seem so..." I trail off, remembering how she counts down when things get overwhelming, how her smile sometimes appears right on cue, like a performance. "...happy."

She turns to face me, moonlight catching in her eyes. "I'm just better at hiding it." The smile she offers doesn't reach those eyes - a perfect demonstration of exactly what she means.

"What do you mean you hide it?" A beat of silence sits between us. I'm fearful that I pushed too hard, but knowing Abigail, she won't answer or talk about something if she doesn't want to.

"Growing up, and even now, I feel like I have to put this mask on that I'm okay. I struggle with my anxiety and depression more than most realize. I am just used to pretending like I'm fine, so I don't make people worry or think less of me."

I tuck a strand of hair behind her ear, my fingertips lingering against her skin. "With me, you can just be. All of you - even the parts that ache." She doesn't speak, just nods, but something in her eyes softens.

"Remember how I used to think you were just some brooding jerk with a pretty face?" She traces a pattern on my chest, her voice lighter now. "Turns out you're just guarding something worth protecting." She's steering us away from the heaviness, and I follow her lead.

"Keep that revelation to yourself," I murmur against her temple, breathing in the scent of her shampoo. "I've got a reputation to maintain."

"What do your tattoos mean?" Her fingers start to trace the black ink across my skin, showing more focus on the rose placed on my left hand. Some of my tattoos have meaning, and some were just stupid decisions made when I was drunk or high in college. When I look at most, a memory pops into my head, but some of them hold nothing in return.

I run my thumb over the rose tattoo, feeling the slight ridge of scar tissue beneath the ink. "The rose grew over what was broken. Some drunk idiot's face versus my knuckles—the knuckles lost."

Her fingertip traces the outline of a petal, lingering where the stem curves. "And what did the other guy do to deserve it?"

Shit. Why didn't I lie? "Oh, well, I got in a fight with my old buddy when I caught him in bed with Charlie's mom when we were in college." The night flashes through my memory. Thinking back, I wouldn't have covered up the scars but instead left them there for me to stare at each day. Maybe it would have kept reminding me how bad Anna was for me.

Her bright eyes widen, trying to decipher whether I'm lying or not. "No shit!" Was that before or after Charlie came?"

"Before." I know people joke that men are stupid. But I think I may be the worst one. "And yes, before you ask, I took her back and eventually got Charlie. Staying was a stupid decision, but if leaving meant I never got Charlie, then I'm glad I stayed."

Abigail leaves tiny kisses on my scars, allowing me to replace the bad memory with one I hope I never forget.

Her fingertip follows the intricate lines of bark etched into my skin. "This tree - you've never told me its story."

I watch her trace the tattoo, feeling strangely vulnerable. "I got it after Charlie came, and my mom kicked all three of us out. One branch is for Charlie, and one is for Bell. I guess I left room in case I found someone down the line that warranted another branch." I proclaim, and for the first time, I wonder if Abigail really could be that next branch.

I can see her mind racing, coming up with questions that she is second-guessing about asking. "Do you want more kids?" She pauses, trying to read if I am upset by her question. "You know, for more branches?" She quickly follows in case I panic over her first question.

My heart hammers against my ribs, but not for the reason she suspects. I shift my weight and swing my legs over the tailgate's edge, the metal cool against my thighs as I stare out at nothing.

"I'm sorry! I shouldn't have asked that. I am getting too nosy." Her voice is hurried while trying to get herself out of the awkward situation.

My chest tightens as I pull her up, so she is sitting next to me. I drag her closer and wrap my arm around her shoulders so there is no confusion if I want her sitting there. "It's complicated." I chew my bottom lip. "I would love to have more kids. But I..."

"You don't have to tell me, Chase. It's okay. Forget I asked." She interrupts me mid-sentence. Her smile is meek, which breaks my heart.

"No, no. I want to tell you. This conversation would eventually need to happen. It might as well be right now." Her head falls to my shoulder as I continue. "I had a vasectomy after Charlie was born." Her eyebrows shoot up in shock. "And not because I didn't want more kids, but because I did."

The confusion on her face is stark, almost comical. I run my fingers through my hair while I try to find the right words. "See, I realized I like the idea of getting someone pregnant too much. Thinking about a woman making me finish in them, and how my sperm could impregnate them, is the biggest turn on. I found the idea too distracting, too consuming, so I had to make it where that wasn't an option."

Abigail's jaw is slack, in shock at what I just told her. I have never actually told anyone that. Not many even know I had the surgery outside of Bell because I needed her to help more with Charlie for a little bit. Did I tell her why? Absolutely not. I don't think any sister needs to know that about their brother.

Her lips curl upward, releasing the tension in my chest. A soft chuckle escapes her, growing until her whole body shakes with it. "So, what you're saying is," she manages between breaths, "you're turned on by the idea of making a woman pregnant? You have a breeding kink?" The lightness in her voice catches me by surprise.

Heat crawls up my neck to my face. "Yeah, I guess if that's what it's called."

"That's..." she bites her lower lip, eyes darkening, "incredibly sexy." As she says it, unbidden images flood my mind—her belly swollen with my child, my ring on her finger. The possessiveness that surges through me is primal, absolute.

She grins, and I feel her warmth wash away every lingering doubt. "Are those reversible?" Knowing she is thinking about that makes me smile.

I pull her over my lap, making her straddle me again. I push her curls out of her face to take in each detail. Her eyes are warm as they stare back at me. I tip her head to the side, showing off her neck for me to kiss and lick. "Yes, Sunshine." I kiss it again as I slide my hand up her legs and make the loose fabric bunch up around her waist. "If I were in a situation where another baby was wanted, I would get it reversed." Her breath catches as I glide my tongue from the bottom of her neck and up before I make my way to bite her earlobe. "But only if my wife wanted me to, of course." Her hips rock against my shaft. Looking into her eyes, I know I have no intention of having this conversation with anyone other than her. And that thought scares the hell out of me.

She arches into me, the soft curves of her breasts spilling over her neckline. I press my lips to that delicate boundary between fabric and skin, tasting salt and sweetness, claiming her with a mark that will bloom by morning. Her fingers tangle in my hair, tugging just enough to make my scalp tingle. In one fluid motion, I'm on my feet with her wrapped around me, laying her down against the cool metal of the truck bed. My fingers fumble with my zipper as she whispers, "We should revisit that conversation soon," while gathering her dress higher on her thighs. Something in her gaze - hungry, unguarded - tells me everything is about to change.

I grind the thick head of my cock against her slick pussy lips, a growl rumbling in my chest as she gasps. She's soaked, her juices already dripping down her thighs. I lift slightly, about to reach for a condom in my back pocket, but her hands stop me.

"Don't you dare," she pants, her eyes lock onto mine. "I want you raw. I want you to fill me up, Sir."

A wicked grin spreads across my face. "You want me to breed this pussy?" I growl, daydreaming about the moment I actually get to do this. My hand wraps around her throat, squeezing just enough to make her eyes roll back.

"Yes, Sir," she chokes out, her hips bucking against me. "Breed me. Make me your good girl."

Grunting, I continue to drive cock into her with one brutal thrust. She screams, her back arching off the bed. "Fuck, you're tight," I barely grit out, drawing back and slamming into her again.

Her pussy ripples around me, gripping my shaft with no plan of letting it go. He leans down, biting her lower lip before thrusting his tongue into her mouth, claiming every part of her. She moans into his mouth, her nails clawing at his back.

He breaks the kiss, his hand still around her throat. "Look at you, taking my cock like a good little girl," he praises, increasing his pace. His balls slap against her ass, the sound echoing through the open landscape.

She whimpers, her eyes watering from the intensity. "More," she begs. "Give me more."

A savage grin splits my face as I pull out, my cock glistening with her juices. I flip her over like a ragdoll, my hands rough and demanding on her flesh. Grabbing a thick handful of her hair, I force her onto her knees, her ass presented to me like a fucking prize. I can see her pussy, swollen and gaping, just begging for more.

"Fuck, you should see yourself," I growl, my voice low and hungry. "On your knees, ass in the air, like a good little slut." I run the head of my cock along her slit, coating myself in her wetness, teasing her clit until she's squirming.

"Please," she begs, trying to push back against me, but I hold her firm, making her wait.

"Please, what?" I demand, giving her hair a sharp tug.

"Fuck me," she pants, her breath coming in ragged gasps.

I laugh, low and dirty. "Oh, I intend to, sweetheart. But first..." I lean down, my body covering hers as I wrap a hand around her throat, pressing lightly. Her pulse flutters against my fingertips, and I can feel her breath hitch. "First, you're going to thank me for every inch of this cock."

I straighten, my hand still tangled in her hair as I press the head of my cock against her entrance. She's dripping wet, her body ready for me. I plunge in, one hard thrust that fills her completely. She screams, a sound of pure, primal pleasure that goes straight to my balls.

"That's it," I grunt, pulling out only to slam back in. "Scream for me. Let me hear how much you love this cock."

Her hands fist the blankets, knuckles white as I set a brutal pace. Our bodies slap together, the sound obscene and filthy and fucking perfect. I can feel her pulsing around me. As she hits her climax, her cunt squeezes me so tightly, my eyesight falters, my cum spilling into her brings me back to reality.

Our breaths are heavy, but when I pull out of her, I see my hot cum pouring out of her. My primal instincts direct me as I push it back into her pussy with my fingers. "Keep this in there, don't let any part of me spill out. I want to know you are full of me when you fall asleep tonight."

Her cheeks blush as she turns towards me. I help her down and smooth out her dress before zipping up my pants. This woman wanted me to make a mark on her, but what she doesn't know is that I have marked her as mine, and there's nothing she can do about it.

Without hesitation, I pull her into my arms and kiss her. Underneath the Texas stars, I realize I may love her.

Chapter Twenty

CHASE

The past couple of weeks have felt like I'm pushing through – every hour piled on top of the last, and I can barely catch my breath. Abigail's soft laughter and warm hand in mine have been rarer than I'd like; our stolen date nights, always too few, drift through my mind like precious postcards I can't stop rereading. Now that Charlie has given her blessing, I can whisk Abigail off to dinner, wind the truck down dirt roads for late-night drives, and even slip my hand into hers when we're alone in the dark. It's a freedom I've been craving.

"Charlie!" I call down the hallway, my voice echoing off the pale walls. "We have to go – Bell's waiting at Redbirds." I know I can't see her face, but I hear the low-toned sigh and the faint roll of her teenage eyes. Honestly, I can't wait for this moody "almost a teenager" phase to subside. Abigail assures me it will, but I pay for my patience as it holds out.

Bell's been hounding me about a lunch date for weeks, but between her packed schedule at the animal clinic and my double shifts to build up a nest egg, we've barely had time to text.

The pounding at my front door shatters the Sunday afternoon quiet. I freeze, listening. Nobody's supposed to drop by today. Probably Lucas or Hayes, I think, already preparing to say no to whatever couch-surfing drama they're bringing this time. The knocking comes again, more insistent.

My emergency work phone vibrates against my hip just as another knock rattles the front door. Perfect timing. I glance between the two, torn for a second before making my choice. "Charlie!" I call out, my voice strained. "Can you get that? I need to take this."

I fumble with the phone, Boss flashing on the screen like a warning light. My stomach drops as I swipe to answer - then freeze mid-motion as a voice filters through the door that turns my blood into ice water in my veins.

A voice like sandpaper scrapes through the doorway. "Hi, are you Charlotte?" I'm already moving before my brain catches up, feet carrying me to the entryway where my suspicions crystallize into reality.

Charlie stands frozen in the threshold, her shoulders hunched forward. "Who wants to know?" she challenges, arms folded tight across her chest as she shifts her weight to one hip - that defensive posture I recognize from our own arguments.

"Your room. Now!" The words come out clipped, brooking no argument. Her mouth opens, then closes when she catches my expression.

My phone wails again. I'm caught in the crossfire - boss demanding attention, stranger invading our sanctuary. "I said now!" The command tears from my throat, sharper than intended. As I answer the call, my boss catches the edge in my voice, and I watch Charlie's retreating back, guilt settling heavy in my chest.

Charlie's eyes glisten with tears. As she brushes past me, I pull her close and kiss the top of her head. I know I owe her an explanation, but there's no time now.

At last, I hustle outside and slide the door shut behind me. I turn to face the intruder, Charlie's mom, Anna – her hand lingering on the doorframe as if she owns every inch of this house. "What in the hell are you doing here?" I roar, daring her to contradict.

"Maybe I missed you," she says, trailing her fingers along my forearm. My skin goosebumps against her touch. She's either here for money or drugs – neither of which I'll entertain. "Are you going to invite me in, or make me a stranger to our daughter?"

I step back, repulsed. "You decided she wasn't your daughter the day you walked out on us. You're too late to reclaim her now. You need to leave." My voice is a whip.

Anna tilts her head, betraying a smirk. "Can't we just talk? Get to know her?"

"You had your chance years ago." I run a hand over my face, trying to calm the surge of anger. "You're not welcome here. Leave."

Her dark eyes flick toward the driveway just as familiar headlights crunch across the gravel. Panic stabs me. I shut my eyes, lean my head back – this can't be happening now.

"Chase, who is that?" Anna's voice slithers into my panic. I crack an eye open and meet Abigail's stare through the glass – her face drained of color. I want to beg her to turn around, flee before this chaos swallows her. "Chase!" Anna calls her tone sharper and louder this time.

Abigail is slowly walking up to the wooden porch to meet me. Her eyes are bouncing between Anna and me as if she knows she just walked in on something. Her warm, summer-dress silhouette makes my heart constrict with guilt and longing. "Anna, you aren't welcome here," I blurt. "What do you need? Do you need money? Fine! How much do you need? Just leave."

Anna's lips curve, venom beneath the honey. "Hmm, I don't think so. Now that I know you have a little..." her voice is dripping with venom as she looks Abigail up and down. "Side piece, I think I'll stick around to stake my claim."

Abigail climbs the three steps and is now standing next to me. Her body language is cold and uncertain, and I don't blame her at all. My instincts tell me to pull her in and hug her. Tell her everything is fine and I'm taking care of it, but if I did, Anna would really lose her temper. She reaches her hand out to introduce herself, but I know there is no point. I don't deserve this woman.

"When were you going to tell me you moved on?" Anna demands. Her voice is rising, and when I see Charlie's silent silhouette behind the curtains, I can only imagine what she has overheard.

I can't help the chuckle that escapes me. "Literally never, Anna." I am shaking my head to keep myself busy, but my legs itch to run. "Honestly, I was hoping I would never see you again." Anna's face is reddening as she takes us both in. "I will give you anything you want as long as you leave and never return. I think you have done enough damage."

I can see her mind wheels turning as she looks at Abigail; she is about to insult her, and I'm not sure how to protect her. "You know, I always knew you would always attach the whores. Some things never change, do they?"

A small gasp echoes around us, and that's when I realize I have to protect the two girls in my life at all costs. "Abigail, will you go inside and grab Charlie? If you can pack a couple of days of clothes and grab her school bag…" My voice cracks. "Have her stay with Bell until I call, okay?" I squeeze Abigail's hand, my voice a desperate plea.

"Yes, of course," she nods, confusion mingled with trust shining in her eyes. She steps inside as I close the door behind her. When it comes to Anna and me, there is nothing to worry about.

Turning back to Anna, I force a polite mask. "I'm sorry I got frustrated. I genuinely wasn't expecting you. My tone is syrupy; my stomach is in knots. "Are you okay? What do you need?"

Anna shifts her weight, arms folded across her chest like a shield. "Thought it was time to reconnect with Charlotte," she says with a casual shrug that makes my blood simmer. Then she glances at her feet before meeting my eyes again. "Plus, my landlord changed the locks yesterday. I need somewhere to crash until things stabilize."

"Ah, there it is." I fight to tamp down my frustrations. "I knew there was more than that." Now, the biggest question is how I will handle this situation. I want to keep her away from Charlie at all costs. "You can't stay here, but I will pay for you to stay at the motel in town."

Her jaw drops. "How will I spend time with Charlotte if I'm never around?" Anna balks back at me.

"You won't," I say, surprising even myself. "Not until I know you're serious about staying – and not coming and going on a whim."

Our stand-off lasts for a few beats before her body visibly relaxes as soon as she realizes she won't win this fight. "Okay, I get it. I will play your game so you can see I'm being serious." Her words have a bite to them, but knowing Anna, nothing she says is real.

I nod, swallowing the mixture of relief and resignation. "Fine. Get your things. I'll drive you to the motel after I check on Charlie and Abigail."

Inside the house, each step down the hallway feels heavier than the last. I pause at Charlie's doorway, watching them sitting cross-legged on the carpet with colorful Uno cards splayed between them. Their laughter cuts short when they notice me standing there.

Charlie gracefully sets her cards down as she looks up to me. "Dad, who is that? How did she know my name?" Her wide eyes search mine.

No time like the present, I assume. I take a seat next to her and explain who Anna is. Her facial expressions are a mixture of uneasiness and fear. I don't blame her because she has never known this woman, and now she is being thrust unwillingly into this new situation.

***

Three weeks later, our routines have settled back into something resembling normal. Anna stays in that rundown motel – far enough from our home that Charlie barely sees her in town. Abigail has reported that Anna has stopped by the library multiple times; luckily, Charlie hasn't been there when this happened. Anna hasn't lashed out at Abigail yet, but it is definitely making Abigail nervous. I can see the tension in Abigail's shoulders whenever she mentions Anna's name.

Tonight, I've carved out one evening for just Abigail and me. We step into Meryl's, the low hum of conversation and the twirl of lights washing over us like a promise to escape. We're halfway through our third slow dance when a swirl of commotion erupts near the bar.

I have big plans for us after we leave the small-town bar and head back to her house. Her thin sundress and boots are screaming at me to peel off of her as soon as I get her alone. All of those plans go crashing down as soon as I hear a commotion towards the back of the bar. Both of our heads swivel in that direction as I realize Anna is in the circle of the loud noise. My heart lurches as I recognize the figure at its center – Anna, surrounded by a rough-looking crows.

"Go. I will be here when you get back." She places a light kiss on my cheeks and turns away, heading to our group of friends sitting against the wall.

I weave through the crowd, voice raised: "Anna! What are you doing?" The group parts, revealing Anna bristling as one young man shoves her. "You were stealing from us!" he accuses, arms crossed.

Dead floods me as Anna clings to me like a magnet. I push her free, exasperation fueling me. "I thought you said you were sober." My voice is flat, more accusatory than I should let it be.

"Well, yeah, I am." She is acting annoyed, but I'm not sure why I'm the source of her frustrations when she has been clearly lying to me. "Sober... ish?" Her commitment to her words is far from convincing. I can't believe I believed her.

My heart sinks. The last thing I want is to watch her unravel around my daughter. I take a steady breath and turn away. "Don't ever ask me for help again, Anna." My voice carries through the smoky tavern.

I march back to Abigail, gather her hand, and guide her out the door. The cool night air hits us like a baptism. I'll face the fallout tomorrow. Tonight, I just need to take Abigail home.

Chapter Twenty-One

CHASE

"What happened?" Abigail's voice falters like a candle in the wind. I catch her gaze, fingers stiff on the ignition, and crane my neck to open the truck door for her. The air smells of dust and evening heat, and I can't find the courage to speak. Instead, I shift the truck into reverse, tires rattling over the cracked asphalt.

We peel away from town and head toward the outskirts, down rutted backroads that shimmer in the late afternoon sun. Through the open windows comes the crackle of an old country station – simple melodies that would usually comfort me, but tonight they sound hollow. Without a word, I kill the engine beside a field of sunflowers. Their golden faces lean lazily toward the light, petals trembling in the breeze. I lift one from its stalk and hand it to her, the stem damp from the recent rain. She presses the bloom to her nose, inhales, but I still haven't answered her question.

Perched on the tailgate while our legs swing free, the night's coolness radiates off the metal and cools my calves through my jeans. The sky is bruised lavender, promising dusk. I wrestle the words until they're sharp on the tip of my tongue. "Do you remember when I told you Anna and I got deep into drugs in Austin?" I force my eyes to meet hers, and for the moment, her pupils dilate in that way they do when she's trying to read me.

"Yeah," she says. The single syllable trembles on her lips.

My throat tightens. I rake my fingers through my hair, feeling strands slip through my fingers. "The first day she got here, she told me she was clean." Silence stretches, hot and sticky. "Then she tried to rip off some guys in a bar for pills. When I confronted her, she admitted she'd been lying." My voice is low – like I'm confessing my own sin, one that drags her too close to the wreckage.

Our quiet swells until the only sound is the buzzing of cicadas in the weeds. Abigail's hand drifts from her lap to mine; her fingers tangle with mine, gentle and pleading. She traces the rose tattoo on the back of my hand – her habit when she's trying to soothe me. My chest caves under the weight of her touch. I clear my throat as tears start filling my eyes. "I can't risk you getting pulled into her mess. She... she has a way of taking everyone down with her."

Her thumb brushes over my knuckles. She looks away, and the light fades from her eyes. I tell myself it's to protect her, though a small voice inside me whispers that I'm just scared. I swallow hard. "I think... we should break up for a little while. Just until I can get Anna out of town and make sure Charlie's okay." My voice cracks, and I pray she can hear how much I don't want this in my voice. "I'm not saying forever. I don't want it to last forever. I just need some time."

Tears slip down her cheeks in slow rivers. I bite my lip, fighting the impulse to wipe them away because I don't think it would be fair for me to protect her anymore. I think I'm hurting her too much to be her savior in this moment. She mumbles something I can't make out and slides off the tailgate. Panic bursts in my chest. Before she can take more than a step, I grab her, pinning her gently against the cold truck bed. I cup her chin, lift her face. "It's just for now, Sunshine. I promise." My words hang between us, fragile as glass.

She doesn't argue. I wish she would. At least there would be some kind of emotion. Hell, I wish she would even hit me because that would be something. I drive her home, the streetlamps flicker on as we pass, and when she steps out, she forces a smile that fractures my heart even more. She turns and closes the door before I can say goodbye. The latch clicks, and I sit in the dark, listening to my own breathing and second-guessing my actions. I never thought that her sunshine would dim, but I have officially done that for her.

***

Weeks blur into each other in the empty space I left behind. I had to tell Charlie why Abigail and I broke up. She took it harder than I expected, those big blue eyes welling with confusion as she asked question after question because she "doesn't understand." I answered with rehearsed half-truths stitched together. Because the sad truth is, I don't understand why I had to be put in this situation either. This is why I have always chosen not to date. If you don't date, you don't have to worry about breaking not only someone else's heart, but also your own.

We've stuck to our routine: trips to the Pigeon Lake Library a couple of times a week to keep Charlie involved with her book clubs and groups she enjoys. Library walls echo with hushed conversations and the scent of old paper, as if mocking me for being there. But twice a week, I stand a few feet from Abigail, forcing a smile, pretending everything is normal. She even took unplanned time off right after we split up. It may not have anything to do with us, but I have a feeling it is. And Mrs. Snyder? She hates me more than ever.

We are on our normal drive home, and Charlie's foot bangs the back of the chair. She is more irritable than usual, but I genuinely don't know whether it's because something happened at school or because she's just sick of being around me. Honestly? Same.

"Dad," she says, her voice muffled by the seat, "you're miserable." The words land like stones. Her brow knitted with worry, and for a second, I see the toll it's taken on her. I don't want her to learn that heartbreak becomes a life sentence.

I press my knuckles against the steering wheel, feeling the vinyl's grain under my skin. "Sometimes in life, you don't get what you want," I repeat, my own mantra.

Before I am able to finish my sentence, she is already shaking her head violently. I want my child to have discernment, but maybe not right now. "But she wants you back. She loves you." Her certainty surprises me. She closes her eyes, counts under her breath like Abigail taught her – one, two, three – then exhales. "Are you sure you're not being dramatic?" she asks, and I can't help but smile at her bluntness.

Am I sure? No. But Anna is still in and out of town, but I have been successful in keeping her away from our home and, more importantly, Charlie. "The saddest part about life is sometimes two people are not good for each other. Abigail deserves more than I can give her. At least for now."

Charlie's eye roll is significant. Even she doesn't care about the lies I'm spewing. "Okay, so we are taking the dramatic route. Awesome."

I choose not to laugh because she isn't wrong. "I'm not trying to be Charlie. I just don't know how to make it better."

I park at Bell's house. Charlie bolts from the truck before it's fully stopped. The gravel scrapes beneath her tennis shoes as I trot up her porch. Bell leans against the railing, her hair glinting auburn in the fading light. She grins. "Charlie said you're being dramatic," she teases, stepping down.

I kick a pebble. "She's too smart for her own good." I shrug.

Her giggle mocks me. "So, you are admitting it? I guess you can teach an old dog new tricks."

"You laugh, but one day you may be in the same situation and won't want me making fun of you when you are pretending to be perfectly fine."

Her first raises in the air out of celebration. "Yes! We finally have a grumpy, asshole Chase back." She hits my shoulder, trying to loosen me up, but it just adds to my frustration. "I've missed him. Come on, tell me you missed him, too.

"Nobody misses him." I quip, looking around her property so I don't have to meet her eyes. I've never been a good liar. Right as I am about to ask about the new horse barn sitting on the back of her property line, she starts walking off and waving. I guess this conversation is over. "Don't get her in any trouble. No candy or pop, Bell!" I yell towards her, praying she will listen to me for once.

Bell's statement is clear as she continues to walk away. She throws up her middle finger before telling me to have fun with Lucas tonight.

I pull up to Luke's shop and give a quick, two-finger wave at Macy as I drive by. She sits on the front steps of their porch across the yard, her belly low and round. I have been told she is past her due date and angrier than ever about it, which is why Lucas has been spending as much time as possible in his wood shop. "Hey, man." I welcome Lucas as I walk through the expansive doors.

Lucas doesn't look up from his workbench. "Is she still sitting on the porch steps?" He questions.

"Yep," I say, sliding into a chair. He hands me a cold beer. I twist the cap off, the hiss of carbonation sounding loud in the expansive barn.

He dares to look out the door and confirms my reporting. "If I end up dead, please tell everyone it was her. I swear her death stare will take me out at any moment." He is joking, of course, but I think there is a twinge of sincerity in his words.

We sit around, listening to some old Pat Green on the radio before Hayes shows up with a refill of beer and some pizza. We deal out cards for poker and shoot the shit for the next hour or so. Hayes announces to us that he is about to go on a multi-month rodeo tour across the States. I feel a pinch of regret that I haven't made more time for him while he was here, and that I don't get to watch him ride more often. I make a mental note to try and do that his time.

I shift in my seat as Lucas deals a fresh hand. "So, Chase," he says, the words slow and deliberate, "when do we find out what happened with Abi?"

Ah, the conversation I was hoping not to have with my friends. It's awkward, you know? Men don't talk about things like this. My chest tightens again as I hand Hayes another beer from the fridge. "I had to do what was best for Abigail and Charlie," I lie, voice low, and refusing to make eye contact with them.

"With Anna in town, I couldn't risk dragging Abigail into that chaos."

Lucas leans back, arms crossed. "I don't buy it."

They both look at each other as if to give a sign they aren't dropping it, and it only makes my skin crawl. "I miss you not being an asshole all of the time." Hayes declares as if everyone hasn't been speaking those words to me.

I let a chuckle escape me because I'm in awe. Why do they think it's okay to push me so hard? "I'm sorry you don't believe me on why I did what I did."

"Do you even believe it?" Questions Hayes, still glancing over to Luke for confirmation, they are still going to push me. "Because I don't either."

Running my fingers through my hair to buy time, I eventually look over at both friends. "Listen, I didn't want to do it. But I got scared, okay? I'm a man and can admit I panicked. I don't want to hurt her because of my old actions. I thought I was protecting her... but really, I was protecting myself."

"Now we're getting somewhere," Hayes nods as if he himself came up with the same realization.

"Don't you think that she would have loved you through all of the bad?" pushes Lucas. If anyone understands situations like this, it would be him. Hayes is great, but he has never had a serious relationship. Lucas though? He is the poster boy for second chances and not letting go of the woman you love. "Macy said she isn't okay. Have you actually talked to her?"

I shake my head, the wood grain under my palms suddenly sharp. "Nope, I feel like that isn't the best. Of course, I see her at the library, but other than that, no. I'm keeping my distance." I take a long drink of my beer before playing with the label. This simple task reminds me so much of Abigail since this is always what she did when she felt uncomfortable. We sit in silence for a while. Somehow, the guys knew I needed to sit in my thoughts without pushing me anymore. "I think I just fell in love with someone too late in life. That timeframe passed years ago." I shrug while I reach for Hayes' empty beer bottle to peel the label off that one as well. "I think she was just found too late in life. I can't give her my entire life, so why even try to give her what I have left?"

Both guys sit in silence with slack jaws. Neither move nor say anything, just staring back at me. With each second that passes, I second-guess what I say more and more. Breaking me out of the spinning thoughts in my mind, both men start laughing. "You're full of shit, Chase." Chimes in Hayes. Lucas' laugh is too easy. "You're an idiot," he adds.

I run my hands over my face and lean forward, burying my head in my hands. "I'm not trying to be an idiot."

"But you are," Lucas says softly, his tone changing. "And you're going to regret letting that one go if you don't do something about it." We can jab at each other, but when it's time to be serious, none of us hides from it. As I peek through my fingers towards him, his eyes plead with me.

"I don't know. We will see." I murmur as I look back at my cards. I don't know if I can fix what I broke. But for the first time since I left her behind her door, I feel a flicker – like a sunflower willing itself back toward the sun.

Chapter Twenty-Two

ABIGAIL

slide the heavy oak door of the library shut, it's latch clicking sharply in the quiet autumn dusk. The scent of parchment and polished wood lingers in the dimmed reading room. Mrs. Snyder's desk still sits empty. She keeps calling out sick, but sometimes I suspect she's invented another ailment just to avoid the rattling dust of town. Lately, I've felt the same urge: to curl up in bed and forget the world exists. I shake the thought off as I pocket my keys, their brass rings jingling in a soft counterpoint to the last echoing footfalls down the aisle of forgotten stories.

A soft hum of a melody drifts through my thoughts until a sudden buzz in my back pocket yanks me awake. My phone vibrates insistently, rattling against my spine. Bell's name splashes across the screen in bright letters. Since Chase and I split, Bell and I have tiptoed around each other, gracelessly polite. She made it very clear to me that she thought Chase was being dramatic and that she told him it was a mistake multiple times. That's sweet of her, but if a man doesn't want to stay, I don't want him.

Hitting the 'answer' button, I hold the phone to my ear. A whistle of wind, a pause, and then her breathy voice. "Abs, I need a huge favor." She sounds frantic, tangled in urgency and guilt.

"Of course," I say, bracing myself for what she needs. I can taste the faint tag of worry at the back of my throat, anticipating the disruption to my carefully scheduled evening.

I hear the sigh before anything else. "Please don't be mad at me," she blurts. "I have to rush to help old Mr. Radley save a cow from who-knows-what. I need you to watch Charlie for me." She barely pauses before jumping in to defend her request. "I wouldn't ask if it wasn't an emergency, but it is. And Chase took Anna to rehab... Shit! I probably shouldn't have told you that." Her rambling gives me time to ground myself in what is going on. "I don't know when he will be home, but it shouldn't be too late. Can you help?"

I pause long enough for Bell to question if I hung up on her. My heart is racing, and my mind is screaming at me not to do it. But my heart? My heart tells me that I love that little girl, and it isn't her fault that her dad and I didn't stay together. "Yes," I manage, but my mouth instantly goes bone dry. "Yes, of course. Do you want to drop her off or have me meet you?" I'm going to regret this.

"OMG, you are a doll. I'm not far away, so I can just drop her off." I hear Charlie's celebration in the background, and I'm reminded of how much I missed her.

A list of things I was going to do before this call flashes through my head. "Perfect, I am leaving the library now, and I will meet you there. See you then!" The only thing I can hope for is that Bell gets back before Chase does. Because if not, I will have to face the man who broke me.

Charlie skips up to me as soon as her feet land on the ground. Her beautiful strawberry blonde hair waves in the wind with each leap through the air. "Abs! I missed you. Did you miss me?"

My eyes water with unshed tears as I give her a hug and kiss the top of her head. She smells like the laundry detergent that Chase swears is the better brand. "Of course I did, sweetheart! You want some macaroni and cheese for dinner?"

"Hell yeah!" Charlie shouts, pausing a moment as she realizes she's not supposed to say that, but I secretly laugh because that's her Dad in her. She grabs my keys and runs up to my door, letting herself in.

Turning to look at Bell, I can see the worry wash over her face. "I'm so sorry to ask you to do this." It isn't her fault, and I always try to do the right thing before anything else.

I walk into my house and hear the TV already playing, and see Charlie's shoes already off and lying on the ground. My keys clink in the bowl on my entry table, and I realize I didn't ask Bell if she told Chase that Charlie was with me. Should I text him?

There are no three little bubbles that pop up, nor does he thumb up my text, but there is nothing I can do about it. I refuse to wait by my phone, hoping he'll acknowledge me. Honestly, it's the best-case scenario if he doesn't. I want to keep this a simple favor for Bell; she picks up Charlie in a bit, and no contact with Chase is needed.

A couple of hours pass, and Charlie and I have played multiple rounds of Skip-Bo. Now we are watching a movie while eating all the junk food I had in my house. I hear a ding from my phone and pick it up before I even realize what I'm doing.

I'm not sure what I was expecting him to say. Was there a magic text I was hoping for that would fix all the sadness, pain, and emptiness? That's something to think about later when I take a bubble bath. But for right now, I need to brush my hair and not look like I have been doing the bare minimum over the last few weeks.

Just over an hour later, I freeze when I see taillights pulling into my driveway. I already told Bell that Chase was on his way to my house, so I know it isn't her. Lord, what I would do for it to be Bell... or anyone other than Chase. But when I hear the firmness of the knock on my wooden front door, I know that my dreams were not going to come true.

Glancing over to Charlie, her breathing is deep as she sleeps off all the sugar she ate during our movie marathon. She is such a beautiful little girl. How could anyone just leave her and come back nine years later like her mom did? I will never understand. Standing up, I tuck a blanket around her and tiptoe toward the door. My chest tightens as he knocks again while I reach for the doorknob. Steeling myself, I pull the door open. I am welcomed by a gorgeous, but very tired-looking, man. His hair is tousled, and exhaustion lines his face. I wish I could look at him with the same love as I used to, but I don't know if I can stomach it tonight.

"Hey," I murmur, my voice fractured. "She fell asleep, but she did eat dinner. Sorry I couldn't keep her awake."

He steps inside, his large frame and energy immediately shifting the energy. What was calm and relaxing is now charged, uncomfortable, and electric. I fold my arms as a flimsy shield.

He crouches by Charlie, nudging her gently awake, before he draws her up. "Say thank you, sweetheart."

"Thanks, Abs," Charlie mumbles, hugging me once more. I swallow a sob behind my mask of calm.

Chase notices the abandoned candy wrappers. "How much junk food are we talking about?" he asks with a half-smile. His deep voice sends shivers down my body. There was a time when that voice was like a warm blanket on a chilly night. But now? It feels more like daggers through my heart.

"She had fun," I say tightly. He frowns at me.

"Dad, don't be annoying. We had fun." Charlie nudges Chase while shaking her head at him. I let her arms wrap around me for an extra beat before I let go. I can't let Chase see me so sad, tears trying to spill.

They both walk out the door, and the moment the door clicks shut, all my composure crumbles. I slide down the wall and let the tears come, like hot tracks down my cheeks. I have cried since everything happened, but I haven't had to be in such an intimate setting with him since. It hurts. The pain of loving someone who just couldn't picture their life interweaving with your own is a special kind of torture. From a room full of joy and laughter just thirty minutes ago, it's now silent and empty.

Knock. Knock.

The soft knock snaps me back. I wonder if I'm hallucinating. *Knock. Knock.* My chest tightens again. Gather splinters of courage, I push myself up, wipe my cheeks, and breathe in slow, measured sips of air. I can't fall apart in front of him.

With much hesitation, I open the door to find Chase standing there. His eyes are shadowed with regret, and where before I would have pulled him to me and hugged him, all I can do now is try to force a fake smile.

"Hey," I say softly, "did she forget something?" I ask as I turn to look around for anything to hand him. I'm not seeing anything.

He inhales sharply, shifting his weight on his feet. His gaze meets mine, fragile and raw. For a heartbeat, the world hushes around us. I see the familiar worry in his eyes – the same one that used to make my heart flutter. He places both of his hands on the top of his head, and I know there is something he needs to say, but doesn't know how. His truck is still running behind him, so I'm not expecting him to stay long on my doorstep. "Chase?" At my words, he takes a deep breath and closes his eyes. I can't help but wonder if he has picked this up from me and Charlie, seeing us do it so many times.

We are in a standoff for several seconds before he turns around, walks off, and murmurs something to himself. I'm not sure what comes over me, but I lose all my patience with this man. "If you want to break my heart, break it once so I can heal. Pretending like you have something to say and then dramatically storming off isn't helpful."

"Why does everyone keep telling me I'm being dramatic?" He yells across the yard. At first, it takes me back, but then I remember this is the reality he caused. Plus, he is being irrationally dramatic right now, but I keep that to myself.

"Would you prefer I call you an asshole, or has everyone been calling you that as well?" I quip back, thinking this may scare him off. I can't lie, though, it felt good to say that to him.

Chase starts taking long strides towards me, and before I know it, he is eye level with me, me standing on the steps while he is at ground level. Seeing him eye-to-eye does things to my heart. I refuse to reach out to him and touch the face I love so much. I want his hands to wrap around me one last time. "They have already called me an asshole, so you don't have to." He whispers so low that I think he meant to say that to himself and not where I can hear it.

Shifting my weight to my other leg, my hip pops out, and his eyes travel up and down my body the way they used to. "At least I'm not the only one who thinks that about you." I pause, worried I may lose all hesitations and really tell this man how I feel about his recent decision-making.

Chase slides his large hands into his pockets, and I can't help but wonder if he is doing that for the same reason why I have my arms crossed: we are both fighting the urge to touch the other one. "Did I make a mistake?" He softly asks.

I'm taken aback because I was expecting a verbal stab back, but maybe he means what he is asking. "Depends on how you look at it."

"What are my options?"

I think for a second before I realize I am going full force into how I feel about everything. Counting off my fingers, "One, you want to continue living a completely miserable life, and you had to get rid of me to do that. Two, you never meant to date me and just wanted to hook up. Three," my throat clogs with the emotions I am trying to keep bottled up. "You realize that I love you, and I'm pretty sure you love me, but are just being stubborn because you are afraid."

As hard as I try to hold my tears in, I know they are flowing down my cheeks when he reaches up and wipes them away, just like he used to. My heart melts a little then, and I release more as my lip quivers.

"Do you love me?" he asks, scared of what my response will be.

"Of course I love you." I pause and look at anything that isn't towards him. "I love you, or I guess loved. I should start training my brain that we need to talk in the past tense since that's our future." The words hurt like glass, but nonetheless, they are words I have to say to remind myself of our reality.

"So, you love me?"

"Yes, you dip shit. If you weren't so convinced that I'm just here to ruin your life or make it significantly harder, maybe you would have seen that. Or maybe not. Either way, I'm clearly an idiot for falling for the broody single dad that refuses to let anyone in." My voice breaks as I stare at him and shrug my shoulders.

"I'm sorry, Abigail." If he were the mushy type of man, I would think he was also about to cry.

I shrug once more as I turn away from him. "It is what it is. Have a good night, Chase. Tell Charlie goodbye for me again. I will see you around."

I'm shutting the door as he slides his foot in to stop me. "Abi."

He doesn't even know what he just did, but that one nickname stops me in my tracks. I'm always either Abigail or Sunshine to him. Does he realize he just called me Abi? "What did you say?"

"Abi, please talk to me. Please. Do you want to grab dinner tomorrow so we can talk this out?" His eyes are pleading with me, and it breaks me.

"No. I can't do this juggling act where you aren't sure if you want me to be with me or not. I deserve much more than that." I am sobbing in my hands as I choose myself. I never choose myself; I always want to be the bigger person for everyone... everyone except me. "I love you. I always will, but until you can decide to never flip-flop on me again, I have to say good night and good luck with everything." And with that, I shut the door in his face and shatter one more time as I fall to the floor. Those words hurt, but if I don't say them now, I'm not sure I ever will.

"You're an idiot," Charlie says dryly as I click my seat belt into place. The leather strap tightens against my chest, and I slide the truck into reverse, the engine rumbling beneath my hands.

"I know." My voice is gravelly in the stillness of the cab. Outside, dusk presses in like a warm blanket, and the horizon bleeds an orange-ish pink. I know sleep won't come easily tonight, but I've earned every restless minute.

Chapter Twenty-Three

CHASE

t's been five weeks since I last spoke to Abi. Whenever Charlie has story hour at the library, I'd call Bell or Macy and have them drop her off. They all knew why but never asked me any questions or pushed me on the topic. I've hated this gap between us, hated myself more for being the kind of jerk who doesn't realize what he has until he destroys it. But I needed the breathing room. I needed to get things in order before I tried to get Abi back. She was right when she said she deserved better. So, I have been moving mountains in my own life, so when she took me back, we could go right into that happily ever after.

Charlie is crashing at a friend's tonight, so I point the truck toward town. I could use a couple of cold beers with Hayes at Meryl's. The neon sign buzzes overhead as I walk in. Inside, the air smells of spilled whiskey and sweaty bodies, the low hum of country music vibrating through the sticky floorboards.

I slide onto my usual barstool. The crowd's rowdy, laughing loudly, wiping foam from glass mugs, but I have no appetite for jokes or dancing with any of the women batting their eyelashes at me. None of them will fill the hollow I've built.

I finish my second beer as Bell saunters in, and right behind her is Abi, her hair tumbling over one shoulder like sunlit silk. Hayes is doing his best to flirt with every waitress who comes by, but it isn't until he offers to buy Abi another drink, and she puts her hand out to take it, that he grabs it and pulls her closer to him. Hayes drags her to the dance floor, and right before I start seeing red, I see his hands wrap around her perfect waist, and she starts laughing. I don't know what that fucker said to her to make her laugh that way, but I hate it.

I rise before I can think, muscles coiling, chest tight. One of the guys here tries to pull me back. Nothing anyone could say or do would keep me from removing Hayes' arm from his body. "He's just doing it to mess with you, Chase. Don't go over there." I don't remember anything after that until my hand slammed into Hayes's jaw, the sickening thud, the way he crumpled. Cheers and gasps ripple through the bar. I stand over him, chest heaving, and vision blurred.

"What the hell, Chase!" Abi's voice cracks beside me. Her expression is a storm of shock, hurt, and anger. She's pushing me, calling me every name she can think of. I don't care. Hayes is my friend, and nobody pokes at my world like that. He knows how hard I have been trying over the last few weeks to get everything in order to get her back.

Abi is still pushing and hitting me, but when I turn to her, my only instinct is to pick her up and throw her over my shoulder. She's kicking and screaming, thumping her boots against my back as I stalk out the back door of the bar when I hear Hayes start laughing and telling our friends that "it worked." What a prick. I don't even feel back for my punch anymore.

I storm out the back door. The alley air hits me – garbage stinks of rot and heat. I stumble toward the streetlight, her muffled swears trailing behind. "Put. Me. Down. Chase!" is all she keeps yelling at me.

I halt beneath a rickety fire escape and set her on her feet, her back pressed against a graffiti-scarred brick wall. Her cheeks bloom red in the harsh glow. Her eyes, once green like the grass, flicker with fear and fury.

"Abi, calm down." My own voice surprises me with its gentleness.

"Don't tell a woman to calm down!" she spits. She squares her shoulders, eye to eye with me, though I'm a head taller. The heat prickles on my skin, and I wrench a hand through my sweat-damp hair, praying for a breeze.

Her tirade slows as I step closer. My heart hammers. There's only one way to shut her up. I bridge the gap, press my lips to hers. She goes rigid- then melts, arms winding around my neck. Her breath catches; my world shifts back into focus. I feel her bow into me, the soft curve of her back, the cotton of her dress. My hand trails down her thigh. The faint line of her underwear offers relief – there's still some boundaries, at least.

"Abi." My lips brush her temple. "Sunshine, please listen." I pull back, dial it down to a whisper. Her lashes flutter. The red in her soft eyes softens. "I'm so sorry." Words tumble out before I can shape them. "Can we take a drive?" I finally mumble while I lift her up again; this time, she isn't yelling at me, and I carry her to my truck.

I ease us onto the gravel backroad lined with tall sunflowers, their golden faces mocking me as I pray to find the right words. Prayers that Abi hears what I say and believes me. The scents of earth and blossoms swirl around us as I cut the engine. I rip a bloom from its stem, tucking it behind her ear before extending my hand.

She steps down hesitantly, the sunflower dancing in her hair. The metal tailgate is cold beneath her thighs as I guide her to sit. The sky stretches wide above, stars sparking awake.

I pace in front of her; hands shoved deep in my pockets. She watches, arms folded, one eyebrow arched. "Chase," she murmurs, voice laced with humor and exasperation, "just say it. You've kidnapped me; how much worse can a confession be?"

There she is, always lightening the mood when I know she is dying inside. I smile ruefully and stop. "I had a whole speech planned," I admit, "but Hayes ruined my big moment. So here we go."

Her smile warms me. I draw in a breath. "I messed up. When Anna came back, I panicked. All I could see was protecting Charlie, protecting... us. I forgot to protect your heart in the midst of it all." My fingers drum against my jeans, restless. "I let fear take over, and I pushed you out to keep you safe from my mess. My hands continue to search for something to do as my edgy energy pumps through me. "I was so focused on Charlie; I wasn't able to step back and explain to you what I was going through." I place one hand on both sides of her, making sure she sees how genuine I am. "I was scared. I was scared she was back in town and would take Charlie away from me. I don't know what I would have done if that happened."

Her lashes flutter. She reaches up, touches my face, palms soft against my cheek. It's all the encouragement I need. "I love you," I continue. "I've loved you for a long time but never knew how to tell you. I went back to that mindset where I dropped everyone solely for survival. But when I no longer had your laughs filling my home, I realized I only had a house and not a home if you weren't in it."

Tears quiver on her lower lashes. I brush them away with a thumb. She laughs softly, the lifting sound I've missed so much. "After that night at your place, Charlie called me out, letting me know she thought I was an idiot. And she was right."

I lean closer, "When I got home, I wrote down everything I knew I needed to provide you if I wanted to be with you." Again, she tries to interrupt me. I place a finger over her lips until she nods in agreement. "I took seriously how I wanted you to feel if you were going to be with me. I never want you to think you aren't the most beautiful thing in this world. I want you to know you are loved. Both by me and Charlie. She looks up to you like a mom, and I love that."

She presses her palms to the cold tailgate, trembling. I cup her hands in mine. "I want you in our lives, forever, as our anchor. I want to be that man for you – always steady, always loving. I want to see you smile because you're bursting with happiness, not because you feel you have to. And more importantly, I want to be that person for you. I don't want your smiles to be fake anymore. I want you to smile because you are overjoyed with your life and not because you are trying to appease anyone around you."

I swallow hard. "I want to have babies with you, Sunshine. I want a whole litter of them with your blonde curls and sassy attitude. I want Charlie to have siblings so that she can teach them how to annoy me." My words shock her because, out of everything I have just said, having children is the most drastic. But I mean every word of it.

Her breath catches. She sobs, the sound full of wonder and relief. I pull her into my arms and let her cry against my chest. She lifts her head, damp curls clinging to her cheeks. "You want to have kids with me?" Her voice is soft and full of hope.

I smile, brushing her hair back. "Of course. I've already talked to the doctor about reversing my vasectomy. I'm ready. We'll do it on your timeline, as many as you want."

Her nod is slow, but radiant. I lift my sleeve to show her the tree tattoo on my forearm – its roots and branches etched deep in ink. "I want as many roots and branches as possible. I can't wait to have that with you. I love you, Abi."

She reaches up, fingers tracing the lines of the tree. "Okay." Her whisper carries all the love in the world.

I press my lips to hers, making up for every day, every hour we've spent apart. Then I scoop her up, loop her legs around my waist, and carry her to the cab of my truck.

"Ready to go home?" I murmur into her hair.

Her smile is as bright as a sunrise. "Yes, Sir."

"You're an idiot," I murmur back with a grin as I haul her to the cab of my truck.

Tonight, she came home with me – and this time, I'm never letting go.

Epilogue

ABIGAIL, SIX MONTHS LATER

When I decided to give Chase another chance, a quiet certainty settled in my chest like a sunrise. He teased that he'd never let me go, half-joking – but I sensed the steel behind his grin. I didn't mind, because in that moment I knew exactly where I belonged. The next morning, I will never forget Charlie's astonished expression when she vaulted into Chase's battered pickup – dirt settled in the crevices – and found me in the passenger seat. She swears she wasn't crying, but I caught the moisture in her eyes, matching the tears I'd shed at giving up hope of ever finding my own family. And here we were, a ragtag trio that felt more like home than I'd ever imagined.

"Hey, Sunshine, do you have to work late today?" His voice drifts across the hush of the library stacks, low and warm, as he leans against my desk. I looked up to find him silhouetted by the afternoon glow spilling through the tall windows. He wore my favorite black shirt – frayed at the collar and torn from being washed and worn a hundred times. The faint scent of cologne, a mix of cedarwood and leather, sent a thrill down my spine.

I rise to greet him, planning a quick peck, but he has other ideas. He grins, eyes lighting up, and I titter as I lean in. "Stop it, Chase! Someone will see us," I whispered, flicking his arm in mock admonishment. He captured my wrist instead, tugging me close, his chest pressing against mine. His stubbled jaw hovers by my ear. "Answer my question," he growls, voice rich with mischief.

A rosy heat flames beneath my skin as his beard tickles my neck. Between the tall shelves filled with books and the idle quilting circle – ladies murmur over their needlework – he draws me closer. I tore myself away, glancing around. "Just until they finish up," I said breathlessly. "Once they leave, I can lock up."

I've barely spoken when he pivots around my desk, seizes my hand, and marches me towards the back corridor. Every step makes my pulse drum in my ears. We rounded the corner into the narrow aisle behind the non-fiction shelves - his secret haven when urgency consumes him, and he can't wait to get me alone.

Luckily, I traded my baggy overalls for a corduroy pinafore dress today, the soft, ribbed fabric hugging my waist over a snug turtleneck. With a quick, fluid motion, Chase unbuttons his jeans and slides them down just enough for me to glimpse his arousal. The warm flush in my belly intensifies as his rough hands trace my calves. In one effortless lift, he hoists me until my legs curl around his hips.

"I think we're getting too old for this, don't you?" I sigh in mock protest when I feel him nudge against my underwear. But the thrill in his eyes tells me he believes otherwise. His metal piercings press against me, one by one, and before long, he is fully inside me, warm and solid. My breath catches in my throat as he begins to move, long and steady strokes that press me closer to the edge before I even realize it.

Just as I teeter on the brink of release, his hands slide around my throat in a firm grip. The world narrows: only the rough brush of his palm, the slick slide of our bodies. My vision swims with sparkles of white when he stifles my moans, pressing his palm across my mouth. I tremble as he slows, riding out our shared ecstasy until the last waves of pleasure shiver through me.

He releases me gently, setting me on my feet. His shirt shifts slightly, and I realize something new: a fine, detailed tattoo curling up his hand. "Did you get a new tattoo today? I ask, brushing my fingers over the fresh ink.

Instead of answering, he lightly squeezes my throat again – this time with a teasing gentleness. Confusion flutters through me. "It's a pearl necklace," he purrs into my ear. I frown, blinking. He chuckled low and explained, "When I give you a hand necklace, at least you'll have a pearl one." He nips my earlobe, and suddenly I see it: tiny, perfect pearls intertwined like delicate fireflies across his skin. "No woman of mine should wear a necklace unfit for royalty," he says softly. My heart clenches with warmth at how deeply he's thought of me.

Before I can respond, he guides me back to the front room, brushing a fingertip across my palm to keep me from speaking. "Come straight home tonight. No stops. I need to show you something," he directs, his eyes unusually serious. I nod dumbly, as if entranced. Another tattoo? A different surprise? With Chase, nothing is impossible.

As I'm about to leave, Macy stops by with her and Luke's baby boy, Asher. I can't believe he is getting so big. I need time to slow down, and he isn't even my child. I tickle and coo at Asher while his mom signs copies of her new book to leave at the library. Yes, we are a library, but when your best friend becomes an author, you sell her books right there at the front desk to support her. I don't care that the grumpy men of Pigeon Lake don't like it. Their wives sure do love it.

I ease my truck down our gravel drive, adrenaline still tingling from Chase's late visit. When I step from the cab, the evening breeze teases strands of hair from my ponytail. On the front porch, Chase and Charlie stand side-by-side, faces lit by the golden sunset. Charlie, in her new sweater and jeans, and Chase, still in that frayed black shirt I love so much. Their grins are conspiratorial, and my heartbeat quickens. Charlie's hair was woven into a braid, Macy's expert fingers - evidence that something special was afoot, and she has been around today. Not to sound dramatic, but is everyone around me up to something, or just acting weird?

On the porch step, they bound down and hurries toward me. Chase slides his hand through mine. The glove-soft warmth of his fingers sends a shiver up my spine. "Get in, Sunshine," he says. "I need to show you something, remember?" I climb into the passenger seat, buckling in with her elbow from the back seat, snapping me from my thoughts. As he turns the key, he squeezes my hand and whispers, "Don't ask questions."

Charlie falls silent too; her lack of words may make me the most anxious. She is beaming like the sun. The stereo crackles to life with an upbeat tune that sounds utterly at odds with Chase's usual playlist of bluesy guitar ballads. I gave in to curiosity at last. "What –."

He cuts me off with a squeeze. I fall still. The truck rolls down the familiar winding back roads, golden fields stretching out under a bruised-purple sky. Finally, he turns off onto a rutted lane, and he pulls up to a wide clearing.

We step out onto a plush flannel blanket strewn with glowing candles, flickering in the breeze that rustles the tall grass around us. Overhead, the stars are winking awake. Chase takes my hand and draws me close, the hush of the world falling away until only his voice remains.

"Sunshine, I don't know if you'll ever understand how much I love you." His words tremble with feeling. Charlie clears her throat with a little squeak, and we both laugh through our tears.

"How much we both love you," Charlie chimes in. We both laugh through our tears because she can't help but add her thoughts to every moment.

"You went from my biggest irritant to the woman I can't imagine my life without. A life of laughter, sticky-fingered children, and chocolate cake that you don't like. What started as flirtatious bickering, I now know that you're more than my fun time."

His gaze swept over me like sunrise warming frosted fields. Then, in a staccato of earnest promises, he speaks:

"You are my Saturday afternoons running errands.

"You are my weeknight dinners.

"You are my beacon of hope when I'm feeling down.

"You are the woman I hope my daughter grows up to be.

"You are my first thought in the morning and last thought when I fall asleep with you in my arms.

"You are my Sunshine.

"And the only thing left is you being my wife."

Chase sinks to one knee while Charlie squeals beside us. "Abi, will you be my wife?"

When he says my name, it feels like the most precious word in the world. My cheeks flood with tears as I nod, unable to speak. He rises instantly, lifting me into his arms and spinning me around while our lips meet in a fierce, trembling kiss.

Behind us, Charlie shrieks with delight and dives into our hug circle.

"Dad! Don't forget to tell her the rest," Charlie urges, bouncing on her toes in excitement. I can barely catch my breath.

I'm not sure I can handle any more surprises tonight, but based on both of their smiles, it's a good surprise. My eyes are wide as Chase pulls me close to him. "Do you like this piece of land enough to build our home on it?" His words barely make sense as I try to fathom what he is saying. Build a house?

"You did what?" I ask, unsure if she is making this up.

He is shaking his head, clearly trying to keep up with everything going on and Charlie's recent declaration. "What do you say? I will sign papers on it tomorrow. But if you want to look at other land, we can. I already talked to the owner, so he knows this was a surprise and may fall through." His rambling is adorable. "I was just thinking that we would need a lot more bedrooms for the number of babies you want..." He runs his hands through his hair, his clear sign that he's stressed. I have no idea why he would be.

"I'm not sure I'm the one declaring we have so many children, but I will go with it for storyline reasons." We both know he is the one who has been itching to get me pregnant. He got his vasectomy reversed shortly after we got back together, but since I'm still on my birth control, he hasn't gotten his way yet.

"It would be great if you could hurry, because I don't want to be too old when I finally get a brother or sister." If this child only knew the anguish her dad has been going through. But it was all in due time. I don't want to rush anything, because this is a lifetime commitment and not a temporary one.

We all three take in the sunset falling on the edge of our field, the sunflowers waving around us. This is when I realize these are our sunflowers, our sunset, our everything. He brushes a kiss on my brow as he pulls me closer under his arm.

"How did we get so lucky to end up here, Sunshine?" Chase asks as he takes both of his girls in as we stand around him.

"Well, you were stubborn as hell, and I eventually told you to get over yourself. Then we fell in love." I add, our story flashing through my mind like a beautiful masterpiece. "But you decided to be stubborn again, so I had to remind you to get over yourself." I know I'm making fun of him, but this is our story, and I wouldn't want to change it.

Shaking his head at me, I wonder how long he will think my jokes are funny. "That's a creative way to look at this." He responds, as if my summary was not accurate.

Now, I turn to look at him, wanting to take him in during the setting sun. "You are the one who made this so difficult. I knew we would end up here for a long time."

He places a tiny kiss on my forehead, taking in our future as he pauses. He likes to pretend he isn't mushy, but deep down, he is. "Good thing I listened."

"Dad! Mom! Let's go, it's getting dark." Charlie yells at us from the truck. We both freeze while tears fill my eyes, realizing she called me Mom. It makes my heart swell so big it nearly bursts.

Back home, Macy and Lucas have transformed our living room into a glowing celebration. More candles flicker on tables strewn with flowers; a cake stands proud beneath twinkling fairy lights. We stumble inside to applause and tears – mostly from Macy. My friend hugs me tight. "You're finally getting your happy ending, Abs," she whispers, and I start sobbing all over again. When I tell her that Charlie called me 'Mom,' her tears became heavier.

Charlie, ever so bossy, snorts. "I'm cutting the cake without y'all if you don't come on!" Her determined stomp makes us giggle through the sniffles.

Knock. Knock. Panic quickly rushes through me out of fear that Anna has returned. Chase's quick look at me communicates he doesn't know who it is either.

Chase opens the door to reveal Hayes, his cast leg propped on a stool, face down with pain and uncertainty. His lopsided grin faltered when he takes in the festive scene. "Uh, did I walk into something?" He asks, eyes wide.

Charlie bound over to him with the proud news. "Uncle Hayes! Mom and Dad are getting married, Dad's going to build us a house, and Mom's going to have babies!"

Her rapid-fire report leaves Hayes blinking in stunned delight. Chase tries to jump in before the rumor mill takes over quickly. "Well... the kids are down the line. We have to get married first. But everything else is true." Laughter ripples around the room, the tension lifting like mist. "Anyways, what happened?" Chase's hand slaps Hayes's back, almost tipping him off balance.

Hayes hobbles forward, wincing in pain. "So, do you remember that rodeo circuit I was going to?" He asks Chase, while he and Lucas nod their head in agreement.

"Okay, well, as you can tell," Hayes says, waving his arms towards his knee as if he needed to highlight his new outerwear, "I got hurt."

"I can see that." Chase hesitantly responds but still steps to the side and grabs Hayes' bag. We all stand and watch him as he hobbles towards one of our chairs. "This is clearly not the best time, but can I stay here for a little bit? Just long enough to heal so I can drive to town if I need to?"

Silence falls back across the group. Chase is looking at me with questioning eyes, as if I'm going to tell his best friend no. Chase sighs before turning towards his friend. "I don't know if we have space, if I'm being honest. If we were in the new house, it would be no problem, but we don't have an empty bed right now."

I feel bad for Hayes, who looks even more defeated after Chase delivers the unfortunate news. I'm going through all the options in my head, but before I can come up with something, Macy's voice pipes up. "What if he stays with Bell?" If the room could get any quieter, it would have. Everyone knows that Bell and Hayes are usually fighting with each other. Is this really the best option?

Before anyone can refute this idea, Chase pulls out his phone, calls Bell, and quickly gives her a rundown of me saying yes to the marriage... and land. "Bell, I need a favor from you." I can hear her voice on the other end, but I can't tell if she is excited about this favor. "I know this isn't ideal, but we don't have room." His pause only adds suspense to the already awkward conversation. "Hayes got hurt at a rodeo, can't walk, let alone drive, but we don't have any beds here. You do."

No speakerphone is needed, as Bell yells "no," and it echoes across the room. "I understand you don't want to, but you can even help with his horse. So, it's kind of perfect, right?"

I hear a lot of murmurs on the other end. Bell is clearly giving Chase a piece of her mind, but per Bell's request, Chase puts his phone on speaker. "Hayes, you can keep your horses at my place, but you aren't staying with me. Find another place." Bell sternly declares.

Chase's color drains from his face as his head drops back in defeat. I'm pretty sure if Hayes could cry, he would have right then. All I want to do is give him a hug and make the situation better.

"Please, Bell?" His voice is so quiet that you could almost miss it. "I will stay out of your way."

A few seconds pass before we hear Bell sigh. "No. Not going to happen."

About the Author

Kayla is a single dog mom who lives in Oklahoma. She enjoys reading as much as she can but also loves OU football. When she isn't writing, she is reading and getting snuggles from her dog, Charlie.

Follow me at @thebookishkayla

Acknowledegmts

Firstly, I want to thank every single person who read or bought the first book, especially those who blindly bought it just because they knew me. Each of you made my small, semi-horrific idea real, and I am still stunned that I sold more than one copy (that wasn't to myself, lol), so thank you!

Thank you to all the small indie bookstores that took a chance on me. Whether it was posts on social media, giving me a table at a signing event, or just overall bringing me into the fold of Oklahoma romance indie authors, I appreciate you. When I become a famous author, I will always make sure to come back to those stores that took care of me in the beginning. I've got your back for a lifetime.

One of the most significant parts of this book, for me, is that Abi is really showing more of me, Kayla, as a person and sharing more personal stories and topics that are real to me. Some are true to the story of what happened, and some were dramatized to give a better story; either way, there is a lot of vulnerability in writing those words for the person behind the computer telling the story.

I hope that each of you can find a piece of yourself in Abi, and that sometimes we have to put on that smile when, inside, we want to scream, cry, or run away instead. I also hope that grace is given to me for the parts where I let you in more than I maybe should have. At the end of the day, I'm just a small-town girl who had big dreams and never wanted the statistics of what I should be to dictate who I would be. We all have a story to tell, whether you are stupid enough to put it in writing and sell it to people or not; that is your choice. 😊

This book is also my love letter to '90s and Red Dirt Country music. It's objectively the best ever made, and if you disagree, then I don't know what to tell you. It's the best.

Thank you to my PawPaw for letting my friends and me drive circles in the old peach orchard while listening to music and talking about life. As I wrote about these nights driving around on dirt roads, my mind continuously kept returning to those mindless circles where I learned how to drive. No cell phones. No social media. Just windows down while singing to mix CDs that were carefully curated. As a teen, I thought it was the coolest, but as an adult, I wish I could tell you how prominent a memory this is for me. Also, as an adult, I would like to ask how much money you spent on gas for us to do this? Were you crazy? Obviously, gas wasn't as expensive then, but holy cow. That was a lot of money. I would make the joke that all that money paid off in the long run with this book, but I'm not there as an author yet, so I'd better not. Either way, thank you.

Coming Next

Who's ready for a steamy second-chance romance between a wounded rodeo star and the small-town veterinarian who holds his heart? You didn't *really* think that I would let these two go without a bit of love and spice, did you?

Bell is the sweet-natured yet surprisingly stubborn final heroine in our Pigeon Lake series. She is the softest of them all, but still a firecracker when she needs to be. With a heart of gold, Bell always shows up for those in her inner circle and for the animals (and familiar bull riders) that show up at her doorstep.

Hayes is the charming daredevil whose broken bones force him to bunk with Bell during his recovery. As his best friend's little sister, she should be off-limits, but Hayes has never been good at following rules. Hayes works hard but plays harder. Now sidelined from the arena, it's time for him to lean into security with those around him and plant roots in the town, and girl, that feels like home.

These two may have *fell* early in life, but some sparks can never be snuffed out... Especially with one bed between them and nowhere to hide, those embers are about to ignite.

This is *the* book I have been the most excited to write since I created the series. Save a horse, ride a cowboy, and all that. Those red dirt roads and cold beer at Meryl's aren't going anywhere, so get ready to *Google* "nearest rodeo to me."